# Feasting With My King

## Joy and Hope in the Face of Suffering

By

### Howard C. Hoffman

Copyright © 2003 by Howard C. Hoffman

*Feasting With My King*
by Howard C. Hoffman

Printed in the United States of America

ISBN 1-591608-97-X

Unless otherwise indicated, Bible quotations are taken from <u>New International Version</u>, "NIV." Scripture taken from the HOLY BIBLE: NEW INTERNATIONAL VERSION®. NIV®. Copyright © 1973, 1978, 1984 by International Bible Society. Used by permission of Zondervan.

Other Bible quotations:
Scripture quotations marked (NKJV) are taken from the <u>New King James Version</u>, Copyright © 1982 by Thomas Nelson, Inc. Used by permission. All rights reserved

Scripture quotations marked (NLT) are taken from the <u>Holy Bible, New Living Translation</u>, copyright © 1996. Used by permission of Tyndale House Publishers, Inc., Wheaton, IL 60189 USA. All rights reserved.

Scripture quotations marked (RSV) are taken from the <u>Revised Standard Version of the Bible</u>, copyright © 1946, 1952, and 1971 by the Division of Christian Education of the National Council of the Churches of Christ in the USA. Used by permission. All rights reserved.

Scripture quotations marked (TEV) are from the <u>Good News Translation in Today's English Version</u> — Second Edition ©1992 by American Bible Society. Used by permission.

Scripture marked (HCH) indicates paraphrase by the author.

Xulon Press
www.xulonpress.com

Xulon Press books are available in bookstores everywhere, and on the Web at www.XulonPress.com.

Signed copies are available from the author for $14.00 plus S/H. Order from him at hambage@mindspring.com

# Table of Contents

Time Notations ................................................................. ix
Dedications ...................................................................... xi
Acknowledgments ........................................................... xii
Prologue ......................................................................... xvii

**Part One: Different Yet The Same** ............................... 25

Different Yet the Same .................................................... 27

**Part Two: The Shepherd's Table: Provision for
    All My Needs** ............................................................ 31

Introduction: Who Will Write for Me? ............................ 33
My Questions, His Response ........................................... 39
Prayer for Peace .............................................................. 43
Legs ................................................................................ 45
The Storm ....................................................................... 47
Panic and Peace .............................................................. 51
Higher Ground ................................................................ 53
On Hassles and Peace ..................................................... 57
Midnight Pain ................................................................. 59

Step Back and Praise .................................................................. 61
Tremors ........................................................................................ 65
Midnight Praise ........................................................................... 69
Lament and Praise ....................................................................... 73
Pray On ........................................................................................ 77
Same Ol', Same Ol' ..................................................................... 81
Yet More; What's Next? .............................................................. 85
My Expectation, God's Promise .................................................. 89
What God Has Done .................................................................... 93
No Terror in His Shadow ............................................................. 95
Loss Gives Way to Gain .............................................................. 97
My Certainty .............................................................................. 101

**Part Three: The Lord's Table: Guidelines for**
               **Victorious, Productive Living** ................... 103

Introduction: Towels and Branches ........................................... 105
The Gauntlet .............................................................................. 115
Grow with Me ............................................................................ 117
Choices ...................................................................................... 119
The Garden ................................................................................ 123
My Lystra .................................................................................. 125
On Beard and Keyboard ............................................................ 127
On Vines and Fish ..................................................................... 131
Pleasant Places .......................................................................... 135
Stretching .................................................................................. 137
Compulsing ............................................................................... 139
The Parable of the Horse .......................................................... 143
How Then Shall I Live? ............................................................ 145
The List ..................................................................................... 149
Being There .............................................................................. 151
The Long Road Back ................................................................ 155
Breakfast With Jesus ................................................................. 159

**Part Four: The Forever Feast: Eternal Celebration
and Healing of All My Disabilities**............163

Introduction: Feastmaker ................................................165
The Long Hope ...............................................................173
Living in Two Worlds .....................................................177
Expectation .....................................................................181
The Forever Feast ...........................................................185
Notes ...............................................................................187

## Time Notations

My life journey
from discovery of disability
to adaptation to a new way of living
has not been a non-stop flight from
Disasterville to Adjustment City.
Rather it is an ongoing trek
characterized both by
advance and retreat.
Unless otherwise indicated by the context,
references to elapsed time
describe when the event occurred
in this journey.

# Dedication

To

Pauline, my bride—
    who since 1954 has walked life's
    untried ways with me
    For better, for worse
    In sickness and in health.
And our Lord Jesus—
    who for many years has guided and
    empowered both of us
    In sickness, in health
    In good times and in bad. . .

this book is lovingly dedicated.

# Acknowledgments

Pauline. For over forty eight years we have been a team. You are a very important part of this book. I learned new things about you as you lovingly assisted my work. Your clinical ears listened between the lines. You protected me from myself when I became too intense. I need and appreciate all of those. Even more, you prayed with and for me throughout this entire project.

Dr. Darold L. Hill, Sr. Pastor, Spring Arbor, Michigan, Free Methodist Church. You have encouraged and assisted me as if I were in a very small congregation. You faithfully prayed for me and this ministry. Read the entire manuscript. Critiqued my doctrine. Evaluated my scriptural interpretation. Your preaching saturates this book and my life. I cannot adequately give credit to specific citations. Forgive me if I plagiarized.

Pastor Earl L. Habecker and Steve Rick, my accountability partners. You both have encouraged, challenged, and admonished me. You quickly learned to be there for me in my difficult MS days. I appreciate your helpful ears and hearts as you listened to me read parts of the manuscript.

Earl, you shared your heart as a pastor, helping me share mine as a writer.

J. Mark Hendricks, Instructor, Ashland Theological Seminary. Mark, thank you for that special encouragement that pushed me out of my fear that I was not up to the task of "rightly dividing the word of truth." I appreciate your insight that kept me from potential errors.

My neurologists— Sanford Fineman, MD and Aida Bodour, MD. Sandy, I owe you a great debt of gratitude. Your clinical skills quickly took you to the right diagnosis; your empathy greatly facilitated my initial acceptance of that diagnosis. Aida, when we moved back to Michigan, you rapidly won my respect as you took up where Dr. Fineman left off. I much admire you as a former colleague and current personal physician.

Xulon Press: My friend, Esther Bailey. Thank you for the introduction to Xulon Press. Without you I would not have known of their existence or their quality of product. Tom Freiling, President and CEO. Thanks for thinking "out of the box" and establishing Xulon Press' high tech publishing. You greatly facilitated my entry into the publishing world. Sylvia Burleigh, Acquisitions Manager and Denise Haverkos, Author Liaison Manager. Thank you for your ready answers to my questions and enthusiastic support of my efforts.

Countless Friends. I feel like the writer of Hebrews; time and space prevent me from naming those who have been involved. You prayed for me. Encouraged me. Practiced patience with me. There are more of you than I know.

My Triune God. You have been my God since I was ten years old. During these past ten years You have worked with me as in no time previously. You have comforted me. Stretched me. Convicted me. You commissioned me to write. We have had many dialogues in the night. You sit with me beside my computer. I feel You impressing me with ideas that are way beyond me.

# Prologue

*In all your ways acknowledge Him,
And He shall direct your paths.*
Prov 3:5-6 NKJV

**Prologue**

**A disability can ...**
Forever change the way you live,
Make every activity challenging,
Threaten life itself.

**I know. I have a disability that ...**
Has robbed me of two careers,
Decreases my balance, endurance,
and muscular function,
Increases my fatigue,
Promises to get progressively worse.

## But, God's Word …
Promises provision for all my needs,
Provides guidelines for victorious, productive living,
Guarantees eternal celebration and healing of all my disabilities.

. . .

Twenty-nine years, three months later I still hear her words pounding in my ears, "When you follow the Lord you need to stay very close; He sometimes takes very sharp corners." Alice Taylor, veteran missionary and mother of children separated from her while they were held captive in a Japanese prison camp, wanted to know why my wife, Pauline, and I were not going back to South Africa for a second missionary term. Taking a deep breath and praying as I spoke, I told her why we felt the Lord was leading us to a new ministry. She listened closely and then gave us that advice which continues to guide us.

Thus far, my journey from birth toward heaven has sauntered over gentle rolling countryside, struggled over huge boulders, and threatened my balance as I slid down steep hills. There have been numerous sharp corners. Some can barely be seen from the distance; at least three have drastically altered the direction of my journey. They define much of who I am and what I do.

I vividly remember that hot summer day in June of 1946. As a ten-year old kid, I was confronted by my need for Jesus. Already I had survived many sermons, attended numerous vacation Bible schools, and enjoyed many potluck dinners. I was a confirmed kid of the church. But that day was different. In the morning I felt no need; I could talk my way into heaven. But then the Lord spoke, and I realized for the first time that I needed a Savior. I ended that day a new person. My sins were gone. The direction of my life was changed forever. Within two years I felt God calling me into His work as a missionary physician. Before I was a highschool sophomore, I had planned my college curriculum. I knew I needed to be ordained if I were to follow God's call on my life. I knew I would refuse to date any woman who did not share my Savior and my Call.

"Well, Hoffman, this is it," I said to myself as I looked out the window of the pastor's study and watched my bride and her father stand at the door of the sanctuary. I couldn't tell if she was nervous; I knew I was. I knew we loved each other and were deeply committed to the Lord. I also knew that my life would be forever changed. <u>I was voluntarily giving up my right to plan my own future.</u> I replaced that with the thrill of knowing we would together walk life's untried way. Together we would seek out the Lord's directions in our lives. Together we would experience the pleasures and pains that lay ahead. We came together to this point, but could walk away. That was no longer an option. We felt ready. It's a good thing we did not know that at age 18 we faced the staggering risk of a ninety-five percent chance of divorce.

Thirty-nine years later, we held hands as we listened to my neurologist. The studies were completed, the diagnosis determined. Kindly and candidly he told us that I have multiple sclerosis (MS). There was no doubt. The data all confirmed the diagnosis. He went on to paint a picture of what we could expect. MS would not kill me. It probably would progressively cause loss of function. It could suddenly, and for uncertain duration, paralyze muscles or cause blindness. There was no treatment that could reverse the damage I already had. There was no treatment that would prevent future attacks (There is now treatment that slows the progression for many people with MS). There were treatments that probably would decrease the intensity of the symptoms.

Despite the seriousness of the diagnosis, we left the

office rejoicing. We had feared a yet-worse diagnosis, a disease that promises death within a few years.

Talk about a sharp corner! Our lives together would never be the same again. Within a few months, I would resign my pastoral appointment and be unable to carry out my duties as a family physician. Pauline would give up very meaningful ministries at the conference and denominational levels. We would leave a small church with many challenges that we could no longer take on and move to one where there were many who could minister to us. For the first time in our adult lives, we would not be church leaders. We were thrust into the never-ending reevaluation of the very fabric of our marriage. How do we see each other and ourselves? What roles need changing? How can we support each other as we want when life is unpredictably changing?

Thankfully life is not all sharp corners. On both sides of each of those momentous events there were many others. Some are of special note; others are just the usual day-to-day stuff of living. Some were especially delightful; others were terribly traumatic. God has used all of them. He has pruned us, shaped us, blessed and disciplined us.

Pauline and I were married so long ago it is hard to remember being single. Together we have had many adventures. We have struggled through years of education for each of us to obtain advanced degrees. We have visited the maternity ward four times, the last in a mission hospital in South Africa where I was both the "supportive husband" and the attending physician. We have four special children and three wonderful grandchildren.

Alice Taylor told us to follow the Lord closely. We look back over the road from South Africa to Michigan to Arizona and back again to Michigan. As we do, we experience the pain and the pleasure of the journey: children coming to know the Lord as their own Savior; patients surviving and failing to survive serious illness; our parents' transition from earth to heaven; listening to Pauline sing in the church choir; developing a small group ministry in a local church. Through these and myriad other circumstances the Lord has patiently worked in our lives teaching us to follow more closely. All this time He was preparing us for that next sharp corner.

Since I was diagnosed with MS in 1993, the Lord has been especially precious to both of us. The rain falls on the evil and just alike. When we were struck by this flash flood, I struggled to maintain my balance. I prayed for His peace and comfort. <u>He quietly thundered</u> in my ears, "I have already given them to you. Reach out and grasp them."

The literature tells me that I was supposed to shout out,

"This is not happening!

"Why me?

"God, how can You do this to me?"

I don't really identify with these. I don't know why. Perhaps it was because for over thirty years I had seen so many people snatched from health that deep inside me I knew I too must suffer some day.

I cried out with my own needs, my own questions, my own hungers:

What is going to happen to me?

How soon will I become nonfunctional?

Can God really satisfy me?

Of what good am I?

I was sure my days of fruitful Christian living were over; I was dumped on the shelf. Patiently He is teaching me that my task is to abide in Him. As I do, the fruit will come, and come, and come. It will endure— He promised us that in John 15.

I have heard God's voice drown out the babble of my fears:

> *Come, all you who are thirsty, come to the waters; and you who have no money, come, buy and eat! Come, buy wine and milk without money and without cost.*
> *Why spend money on what is not bread, and your labor on what does not satisfy? Listen, listen to me, and eat what is good, and your soul will delight in the richest of fare.*
> Isa 55:1-2

Walk! Ride your wheelchair! Use your service dog! Call for Dial-A-Ride! Whatever it takes, join me! Bring all of your hungers. Together we can be seated at the King's table. Together we can feast and be satisfied. Sated, if you will. And never forget, the best is yet to be.

> *Now there is in store for me the crown of righteousness, which the Lord, the righteous Judge, will award to me on that day— and not only to me, but also to all who have longed for his appearing.*
> 2 Tim 4:8

PART ONE

# Different Yet The Same

*They feast on the abundance of your house; you give them drink from your river of delights.*

Ps 36: 8

# Different
# Yet the Same

What is the crippled grandson of King Saul worth? Apparently not much. Scripture even introduces him wrapped up in parentheses,

> *(Jonathan son of Saul had a son who was lame in both feet. He was five years old when(the news about [the deaths of] Saul and Jonathan came from Jezreel. His nurse picked him up and fled, but as she hurried to leave, he fell and became crippled. His name was Mephibosheth.)* .
>
> 2 Sam 4:4

Listen to King David's advisors. "Ignore him," urges the Minister of Internal Affairs, "He isn't worth anything to you or the kingdom." "Liquidate him," warns the Minister of Defense, "before an opportunist turns his wretchedness into sympathy for your enemies." "Don't be hasty," commands the king. "Bring him to me."

Imagine Mephibosheth's fear as he stumbles into the king's presence. Notice the tension in his muscles, the hesitancy in his walk, the terror on his face.

Listen to his thoughts, "Why have you brought me here to ridicule me and bring shame to my father Jonathan and grandfather King Saul? Why must you make me a public laughing stock before you kill me?" Listen in astonishment, as he does, when the king speaks,

> *"Don't be afraid ... I will surely show you kindness for the sake of your father Jonathan. I will restore to you all the land that belonged to your grandfather Saul, and you will always eat at my table."*
>
> 2 Sam 9:7

Mephibosheth the impaired becomes a member of the royal family! Before, he hid in fear, now he lives in the palace. The new Mephibosheth still limps on two deformed feet. He struggles to get to the table; once there he feasts on royal cuisine and talks with the most powerful man in his world.

...

Three thousand years later, two physicians discuss the current challenging case. "I will want to do an EMG[1], and almost certainly an MRI[2]. This is not a problem of the hip. Almost certainly we are dealing with a neurological problem. I suspect Multiple Sclerosis (MS). It could be Lou Gehrig's disease (ALS). We will have to wait and see." Doctors talk together like this all the time. This time, however, the presenting physician was also the patient. After months of increasing limp, pain, and fatigue, I had to admit this was more than a problem of arthritis.

I drove the long way home. I needed time to look at my new reality. I'd rather have a bad hip; that can be fixed. My first patient with MS was 20 years younger than I was this day. He had far-advanced disease. His caretakers had neglected him. My brain told me his case was different than mine; my gut refused to believe it. And ALS? I couldn't think of a worse disease. Obviously I knew too much. An EMG? That hurt a little. No sweat. An MRI? To do that you had to go head first into a long narrow tunnel. Only a week before, a patient practically rebelled at the prospect, almost shouting at me, "You will never get me in one of those again!"

I took the really long way home. The Lord and I had a lot to talk about. I needed his peace, his reassurance. The events of the day made it hard to listen. I recalled his precious graciousness over the years. Still, fear grabbed at my throat. The thought of the MRI machine thrust me into a panic. I couldn't do it alone, I positively knew.

A few days later, supported by my wonderful wife and buoyed up by my Savior and Lord, they pushed me head first into that dreadful looking instrument. I didn't know if I could do it. And there I met my Lord. For forty-five precious minutes, the Master of the Universe and I talked. I was genuinely sorry when they announced the procedure was finished. I was ready to face my future.

Three thousand years ago, an impaired grandson of a dead king ate at the king's table in the royal palace. Four years ago, I feasted with my King in the belly of a cold, foreboding medical instrument.

...

In the smallest slice of time, Mephibosheth's life was forever changed. His healthy five-year old legs were twisted beyond the skills of the doctors. His future was bleak, at best— that is until King David projected himself into his life. Mephibosheth still struggled to walk but he no longer feared what life could do to him. He had all the power of the king at his disposal.

Over the course of the next months, I gradually lost the functions I needed to continue my careers of medicine and ministry. In the middle of my pain I was repeatedly invited to eat at the King's table. The meals were free. I, too, had all the power of the King at my disposal.

> *O LORD, you preserve both man and beast. How priceless is your unfailing love! Both high and low among men find refuge in the shadow of your wings.*
> *They feast on the abundance of your house; you give them drink from your river of delights.*
> Ps 36: 6b-8

Then Jesus declared, *"I am the bread of life. He who comes to me will never go hungry, and he who believes in me will never be thirsty."* John 6:35

## PART TWO

# The Shepherd's Table: Provision for All My Needs

*You prepare a feast for me*
*In the presence of my enemies.*
*You welcome me as a guest,*
*anointing my head with oil.*
*My cup overflows with blessings.*

                                            Psalm 23:5 NLT

# Introduction: Who Will Write for Me?

Gazing through your RetrospectOScope, peer over the shoulder of the celestial scribe transcribing a notice to be dispatched to a location in the Judean countryside.

> Needed: A writer of My holy scriptures to proclaim My loving concern, faithfulness, and protection in all of life's experiences. The one whom I appoint will bring to the assignment their willingness to follow Me wherever I lead and can expect to encounter a wide range of pleasant and unpleasant experiences. A sinless life is not required; genuine confession and repentance of sin is mandatory. The person chosen to carry out this assignment must be known as a person after My own heart. David, meet Me at My altar.
>
> Your Shepherd

Psalm 23

*The Lord is my shepherd; I have everything I need.*
*He lets me rest in green meadows; he leads me beside peaceful streams.*
*He renews my strength. He guides me along right paths,*
*bringing honor to his name.*
*Even when I walk through the dark valley of death,*
*I will not be afraid, for You are close beside me.*
*Your rod and Your staff protect and comfort me.*
*You prepare a feast for me in the presence of my enemies.*
*You welcome me as a guest, anointing my head with oil.*
*My cup overflows with blessings.*
*Surely Your goodness and unfailing love will pursue me*
*all the days of my life*
*and I will live in the house of the LORD forever.*
NLT

    The profound simplicity of Psalm 23 has captured my thinking and writing for days. At four-thirty I woke from a deep sleep. Questions whizzed through my brain. Profound emotion filled my heart. My pillow silently absorbed tears of praise.

    What was David doing when he wrote these words? Had he just rescued a straying lamb? Killed an attacking bear? Perhaps he was thinking ahead to the dangerous mountain pass he must traverse with his sheep to their summer grazing. Maybe he was studying his flock as the sheep rushed into the deep lush green of the meadow or waded into the still pool of water.

Then, again, perhaps he wrote these words long after he exchanged the hillside in Judea for the palace of King Saul. Maybe it was yet later when he escaped the wrath of King Saul and lived as a fugitive in the caves of those same mountains.

Whatever the time, wherever the place, David validated the truths of this psalm. For three thousand years, countless people in all of life's circumstances have relived David's experiences and found new hope from these words.

Emotion rushes in as I relive the final hours, maybe minutes, of my dad's life. My mother, Pauline, and some of our children were gathered with me around his bed. We could barely hear as he began to speak. Then we knew he was reciting the Twenty-third Psalm. Together we recited those precious words with him. Together we reaffirmed the promises and again experienced their healing power. Together we dined at the table our Shepherd laid out for us.

I live much differently now than I did that day fourteen years ago. Back then, I provided medical, and sometimes spiritual care for many patients. I was deeply involved in the life of my church. I ventured in life. I enjoyed good health and came to expect it would last for many years. I saw myself more like a shepherd than a sheep.

Then my carefully maintained schedule crumbled. My world view blurred until I could hardly see its landscape. I felt robbed of the opportunities to assist anyone along their life journey; tossed on the shelf; a used-to-be physician and minister. As my vision began to clear, I saw high mountains, deep ravines, dangerous passes, and my Shepherd reaching out to me. I was delighted to be a sheep. I snuggled into the warmth of His embrace. I was content to be led to food and water.

Time marched on. My Shepherd dramatically met my needs over and over. His persistent faithfulness dramatized

His love and power. I am now thoroughly convinced there are no life circumstances that can frustrate, much less invalidate His ability.

Share some of my experiences with me. You will see pain, discouragement, agitation, exhaustion, and sometimes near-defeat. You will also view God's wonderful interventions. Together we can relive our problems; together we can rejoice in His solutions.

# Meditations

# My Questions, His Response

What am I doing here? Why do I still have MS? What is God up to? I don't know; some of my well-intentioned friends seem to. They have offered the supplement-of-the-month cure on four different occasions. "Its all natural and can't hurt you," they said. Perhaps they forget poisonous mushrooms are all natural as well. They all want to see me cured, or at least much better than I am. I appreciate that. "You need to pray," a wonderful friend asserted. "God surely wants to heal you. Maybe there is some spiritual pride that prevents an answer." I asked her to pray on. I need her to pray that God will do His will— not mine or hers. On three occasions I responded to God's nudges and requested anointing for healing. And still the disease slowly inches along.

So what is it that God intends to do? I don't know— He hasn't revealed His plans yet. But then, you know, He didn't tell Job either. In fact, God never told Job that He had given power to Satan who snatched away all his property, killed all of his children and their families, and inflicted Job with major, disgusting disease. Remember how Job scraped his sores with broken pottery? It is enough to turn the stomach of a seasoned physician.

God did tell Job not to play God. Listen to Him thunder out of the storm:

> *"Who is this that darkens my counsel with words without knowledge?*
> *Brace yourself like a man; I will question you, and you shall answer me.*
> *Where were you when I laid the earth's foundation? Tell me, if you understand."*
>
> Job 38:2-4

And again:

> *"Brace yourself like a man; I will question you, and you shall answer me.*
> *Would you discredit my justice? Would you condemn me to justify yourself?*
> *Do you have an arm like God's, and can your voice thunder like his?*
> *Then adorn yourself with glory and splendor, and clothe yourself in honor and majesty."*
>
> Job 40:7-10

Listen as Paul confides the great revelation the Lord gave him:

> *I know a man in Christ who fourteen years ago was caught up to the third heaven ... He heard inexpressible things, things that man is not permitted to tell.*
>
> 2 Cor 12:2,4

Can you imagine the burden that secret heaped on him? How would I manage such a blessing? Apparently I am not alone; Paul had his problem, too. But then, don't take it from me, hear his own confession:

> *To keep me from becoming conceited because of these surpassingly great revelations, there was given me a thorn in my flesh, a messenger of Satan, to torment me. Three times I pleaded with the Lord to take it away from me.*
> 
> 2 Cor. 12:7-8

Read on:

> *But he said to me, "My grace is sufficient for you, for my power is made perfect in weakness. Therefore I will boast all the more gladly about my weaknesses, so that Christ's power may rest on me."*
> 
> 2 Cor 12: 9

My Jesus, I sometimes crumble under the weight of the load— the load that I fail to give to You. I don't need to know Your plans regarding my physical health. I already know You yearn with all Your love to bring me closer and closer to You. Help me to keep faith with Your agenda. I long to say with Paul:

> *"That is why, for Christ's sake, I delight in weaknesses, in insults, in hardships, in persecutions, in difficulties. For when I am weak, then I am strong."*
> 
> 2 Cor 12:10

That is enough.

# Prayer for Peace
⇒•⇐

Lord, listen up. You need to listen to me! Don't You hear me?

The Lord needs to listen? What a ridiculous thought. Of course He doesn't need to listen. Still I have to shout out my pain. I cannot hold it in any longer. Pauline and I have held each other and cried together until we could cry no longer. We have prayed together over and over as we have faced this sharpest of sharp corners. We feel jerked around this one. We know we cannot make it different. We are scared. What is to happen?

Father, I must tell You where I am coming from. I need for You to hear. I know that, without Your miraculous intervention, I face a future of progressive loss of function. My relationship with Pauline can never again be the same. What kind of a husband can I be for her? How much is she going to have to carry of my load?

Fatigue paralyzes me; I can't work. Will I ever be able to go back to the patient's bedside? I have had over thirty wonderful years helping thousands of patients. If I have to, I can give that up. With help from You and Pauline, I can plow my way through that.

Ministry? That is altogether different. You recently granted me the privilege of active professional ministry. We have worked together to develop a vigorous small group ministry in a local church. I can no longer support these wonderful new leaders. I have had to lay it aside, drop it on the scrap heap. That was terrible. Intolerable.

What about the future? I know too much. I know that MS gets worse and worse. Lord, what are Your plans? Are You going to heal me or do I need to learn to face a future of progressive losses?

All of these concerns pound in my brain and heart. I can lay them aside for only the briefest of time. My pain incapacitates me. I even find it hard to expand my concerns to include my precious wife. I am frozen. Immobile.

Speak to me, Lord. Tell me You have it all under control. I have known for dozens of years that today's concerns are plenty. I know Your love and care for me vastly exceeds my wildest anticipation. But I need to know that in a new way. I need to tell You how much I am depending on You to take care of this whole rotten mess.

Jesus, just hours before You died, You certified that You have given me all the comfort and strength I need:

> *Peace I leave with you; my peace I give you. I do not give to you as the world gives. Do not let your hearts be troubled and do not be afraid.*
> John 14:27

I cannot appropriate those just now, Lord. I am too numb. Enable me to reach out with the faith You have given to grasp the gifts You have already granted.

# Legs
※

Six months ago my brain thrust me forward into my medical future as if it had already occurred. Painful limp. Corrective surgery. Intensive rehabilitation. Decreasing discomfort. Functional recovery. How many times had I seen that process repeated in the lives of my patients? I don't know. I don't collect statistics; I spend my energies treating real people with real problems. Over the last months my good friend and colleague went through this process. And now he skis again.

Six weeks ago I relearned the centuries-old adage, "The person who sees their doctor in the mirror has a fool for both physician and patient." My doctor rewrote my medical future. There is no corrective surgery. Unless the Lord miraculously intervenes, I will limp more and more until some day rather than walk I will sit out my days in a wheelchair. My natural optimism and an I-can-do-it mentality have been jerked out of my personality. In their place are pessimism and crushed self-esteem.

Today God dazzled me with Himself. The words are so bright they threaten to ignite the page of scripture. Look for yourself:

*His pleasure is not in the strength of the horse,
nor his delight in the legs of a man;
the LORD delights in those who fear him,
who put their hope in his unfailing love.*
Ps 147:10-11

I have walked with the Lord for forty-seven years. I haven't the faintest idea how many times I have read these words. Today, I claim them for myself. More than that—they grasp me. And grasping me, they will, over time, restore my optimism, reshape my self- esteem, move me ever closer to my Master. I cannot feel these assertions. By faith I claim them.

# The Storm

As if trapped in a stationary front, the cloud had engulfed me for weeks. Fear thundered in my ears. Uncertainty flashed grotesque images of my future. The storm drowned my usual optimism. I felt like a lonely child caught in a sudden downpour at night. The Lord and my wife, Pauline, were always there, but I could not really hear or see them. I was too preoccupied with my problem-drenched self. Comfort and reassurance seemed so far away.

Despite my skill as a physician, I hadn't had the faintest suspicion of an impending storm. For as long as I remembered, I had enjoyed the clear skies of good health. There was only the occasional cloudy day. But the clouds began to gather on that fateful day when the neurologist told me he thought I had more than a simple problem of an irritated nerve in my left thigh. The sky darkened as he talked of unpleasant tests to identify the problem. I heard the first clashes of thunder when he told me what he suspected. The clouds let loose a deluge of rain. Lightning! Thunder! Rain! More lightning, thunder, and rain. It seemed it would never stop.

Despite my many years of commitment to Jesus Christ, I was unable at first to find any comfort from scripture or prayer. Jesus' command

> *" ... do not worry about tomorrow, for tomorrow will worry about itself. Each day has enough trouble of its own."*
>
> Matt 6:34

seemed impossible to follow. The Lord was out of sight, out of hearing. Despite many years of a wonderful marriage to Pauline, she seemed distant. I struggled to know she was really there. I felt terribly alone.

Listen with me to the anguished cries of Jesus' disciples in the middle of their storm.

Jesus had said,

> *"Let's go over to the other side of the lake." So they got into a boat and set out.*
> *As they sailed, he fell asleep. A squall came down on the lake, so that the boat was being swamped, and they were in great danger."*

*The disciples went and woke him, saying,*

> *"Master, Master, we're going to drown!' He got up and rebuked the wind and the raging waters; the storm subsided, and all was calm ... In fear and amazement they asked one another, "Who is this? He commands even the winds and the water, and they obey him."*
>
> Luke 8:22-25

My Master's voice broke through the thunder and wind that threatened me. Howling wind and crashing thunder are no match for Jesus. He spoke; they fell at His feet. In the peace that followed, I knew I was not alone. I heard Jesus' still, small voice and Pauline's tender whispers.

I thank you, Polly, for your tender love, your patient understanding.

I praise You, Lord Jesus, for Your power and Your love. I pray that in the storms that lie ahead I will remember this experience and that, in remembering, will look to You and not to my circumstances.

# Panic and Peace
❯•❮

Peace. Quiet. A soft glow from the night lights. Everything predicted a great night's sleep.

Pauline and I had just turned out the lights and were settling down to close off a good day. I was almost asleep—only vaguely aware of my surroundings. Dreams brushed against my consciousness.

But then— Zing. Smash. It clobbered me again. Suddenly the room was too small, too dark.

My covers crushed and constricted me. My emerging dream exploded into a nightmare. How many times has it happened? I don't really want to remember. Far too many by any account.

For over five years recurring episodes of agitation and panic have suddenly interrupted months of peaceful living.

During these episodes I have reconfirmed lessons learned from a near-lifetime of walking with Jesus, forty-five wonderful years of marriage to my teenage sweetheart, and thirty years of medical practice. I call the treatment plan the Therapeutic Three. The order of application varies from time to time. Sometimes one will do; often I need all three. Let me illustrate from the last eruption.

Watch as I struggled to get out of bed— anywhere to find more light, more space! Listen as Pauline offers to talk with me. Join us as we play a few hands of Rummy. Feel the tension gradually subside. Phase one seemed successful as I started back to bed. But first I needed to introduce phase two. For all these years, I have been on medications that control a host of MS symptoms. Sometimes those need adjustment. My physician and I have developed the rules for me to make adjustments. I take the appropriate medication and climb back in bed. After a whole thirty seconds (give or take a few) of peace, the monster strikes again. I vault out of bed. It is time for phase three. It's time to talk with Jesus. I listen for His voice. I read.

I pray. I feel the nudge to once again visit 2 Corinthians chapter twelve. Once again I hear the Lord Jesus talk with Paul in the face of his storm:

*"My grace is sufficient for you, for my power is made perfect in weakness."*
                                                                2 Cor 12:9.

My weaknesses. I sure demonstrated them tonight! His strength. I didn't need convincing. I've experienced it for years. I grabbed hold of that promise like a struggling, panicky swimmer grabs the offered rope.

Peace. Quiet. A soft glow from the night lights. I snuggled under my covers, thanked my savior, embraced my wife, and gently dozed into my first dream of the night.

# Higher Ground
❧•❦

> I want to scale the utmost height
> and catch a gleam of glory bright.
> Though some may dwell where fears abound,
> My prayer, my aim is higher ground.
> (Selected phrases)

Our devotional challenged us with that hymn on March 20, the day I turned sixty-one. Birthdays! When I was a child at home, we celebrated life and growing up. Now I celebrate the successful completion of the previous year and the anticipation of what this new one will bring.

The last four years have been a roller coaster ride with exhilarating ascents, gut-wrenching descents, dizzying twists, and even some belly-up panics. The Lord has always ridden with us, celebrating, comforting, stabilizing, and protecting. I am amazed at how wonderfully Jesus matches challenge with strength, danger with protection, and turmoil with peace. These four years leave me overwhelmed by his love, grace, and power. They also leave me exhausted. I have minimal reserve and that reserve is quickly used.

Now for next year ...

"Scale the utmost height?" How about sitting on a mole hill?

"Catch a gleam of glory bright?" I'd rather protect my eyes.

"Though some may dwell where fears abound." I sure don't want to do that.

"My prayer, my aim is higher ground." First I need some energy!

Maybe if I put everything I have to it, I can pull myself up enough to lie on the floor. Maybe I can get up enough optimism to believe I will make it until noon. Maybe I can find enough energy to pray. Absolutely, totally, indisputably exhausted. Ugh!

But then my mind turns to God's promise for the resources I need. Somehow the Lord thrusts two great passages into my mind. They have both rescued me in the past. With God's help, I'll test them again. Now!

> *Even youths grow tired and weary, and young men stumble and fall; but those who hope in the LORD will renew their strength. They will soar on wings like eagles; they will run and not grow weary, they will walk and not be faint.*
>
> Isa 40:30-31

As if that were not enough, there is more:

> *So Joshua fought the Amalekites as Moses had ordered. Moses, Aaron, and Hur went to the top of the hill. As long as Moses held up his hands, the Israelites were winning, but whenever he lowered his hands, the Amalekites were winning. When Moses' hands grew tired, they took a stone and put it under him and he sat on it. Aaron and Hur held his hands up— one on one side, one on the*

*other— so that his hands remained steady till sunset. So Joshua overcame the Amalekite army with the sword.*

Exod 17:10-13

How can I thank him enough?

Even as I write, my greatest support and wife of a million wonderful years comes home from yet another task. Right on her heels, a dear friend comes by checking on my progress. Thank you Lord for a helper on either side!

Now, where is that mountain?

# On Hassles and Peace
❧•❦

Oh, for a calm, quiet day! But that was not to be. Confusion. Too many stimuli. Ceaseless interruptions. My strength fails to meet all those demands. The hassles of life inflict their penalty. *Hassle.* My dictionary tells me the word is old; it originally meant "To hack at, cut with a blunt knife and with a sawing motion." [3]

I came to my study looking for a quiet time to hear from the Lord. "Lord", I said, "What is Your word for me today? I need to hear from You, I need to see Your face." I listened. I pondered. I heard nothing. I tried a word search in my Bible software. Still nothing. And then the doorbell rang. Yet another interruption!

His name is Joe. He came to service my stairway chair lift. After describing potential problems, I returned to my "solitude." I pondered. I listened. Nothing. And then he called me back to the stairway. He reviewed his work. He asked for his check. And then he noticed a picture on our wall— a little girl is sitting on her sled; a bird sits on the limb of a tree. I have seen this picture for years. It reminds us of our two now-grown daughters. But Joe saw something I had seen but never really noticed. "Her eye is on the little bird," he said and then God thundered in my ears with Joe's next words, "His eye is on the sparrow." That's all he said. To me it was the voice of God Himself. Using a previously unknown Christian brother, He cut through the clutter of the day. I heard Jesus say,

> *Are not two sparrows sold for a penny? Yet not one of them will fall to the ground apart from the will of your Father.*
> *And even the very hairs of your head are all numbered.*
> *So don't be afraid; you are worth more than many sparrows.*
> Matt 10:29-31

I returned to my desk. Even as I type these words, the interruptions continue. It's the phone this time. More of the same yet altogether different, God's voice rises clearly above the din in my environment. I hear his voice reminding me once again,

> *Never will I leave you; never will I forsake you.*
> Heb 13:5

Life is no longer tearing at me. Jesus's peace destroys the hassles.

# Midnight Pain
⇒•⇐

It's 12:30 in the morning. I ache. I hurt. I'm tired. I can't sleep.

So, I just suffer alone, right? Wrong! The psalmist had suffered, too. In the midst of his agony he reminds us,

> *By day the LORD directs his love, at night his song is with me— a prayer to the God of my life.*
> Ps 42:8

The prophet Elijah, in the middle of his despair at the threat against his life, was fed by an angel, visited by God in the "still small voice," and strengthened for new service (1 Kings 19).

I cannot avoid all the pain of life. I can know he is with me and meets my needs. The pain may persist; his song certainly will. I need to listen for the song and the still small voice. With the Psalmist I can affirm,

> *Why are you downcast, O my soul? Why so disturbed within me? Put your hope in God, for I*

*will yet praise him, my Savior and my God.*
Ps 42:11

As Elijah went from the cave to anoint two new kings and appoint Elisha as his own successor, so can I be strengthened for new challenges for my Lord.

And now, I think I will be able to sleep.

# Step Back and Praise

Yesterday was one of those days. It started well. I spent time with my Lord in study and worship. I finished several needed tasks. And then ... IT happened.

We had gone to the mall to get birthday gifts before tomorrow's family celebration. You remember Jesus said that the rain falls on the just and the unjust alike? Actually that says it mildly! Rain? Try tornado! IT struck in a nearby town. We, with all the rest of the mall-shoppers, spent forty five minutes in a narrow shelter — until the tornado chose to move on.

I was stressed, overheated, fatigued. And the day was not over yet! Our granddaughter's school program was yet to come. I survived that. And then I was not just tired, I was drained. Shot. Wiped out. Insensible.

Prostrate from yesterday, today started at low and went down from there. Maximal things to accomplish; minimal energy. Maximal demands — all of very high priority. Maximal frustration; minimal effectiveness! Need I say more?

So what to do? The Lord is teaching and I am slowly earning that "maximal tasks plus minimal time and energy" equals overwhelming need to step back, consult God's Word, praise Him for who He is, and spend time with Him in prayer.

That goes against all the wisdom of the world: "When you are in the time-and-task crunch, cut out all the unnecessary, get on with the tasks at hand. God will wait for you. Now is the time to work, not worship." You know, when I see these words I have written, it seems so obviously wrong; I discover the error only when I stop, step back and get the Lord's point of view. How many times have I nearly exploded with frustration because I unthinkingly followed the conventional wisdom of the world? How much of God's refuge and strength have I missed? As Ps 46 tells us so poignantly:

Our great God

> *... is our shelter and strength,*
> *always ready to help in times of trouble.*
> *So we will not be afraid, even if the earth is shaken and mountains fall into the ocean depths;*
> *even if the seas roar and rage, and the hills are shaken by the violence.*
>
> vv 1-3 TEV

He reassures us.

> *The LORD Almighty is with us;*
> *the God of Jacob is our refuge.*
>
> v 7 TEV

By faith I believe all the above and claim them for myself. Therefore, since God is bigger than "what's the matter," I can relax, stop fretting, and remember that He is still my God; He still holds the reins on this world of mine. I will commit all my days and all my activities to Him. I no longer have any reason to be harried when I do not accomplish all that I would desire in a day.

# Tremors

Tap. Tap. Tap, tap. Tap. Tap, tap-tap. With a rhythm all its own my left thumb beats against its neighboring index finger.

Jump. Jump,jump-jump-jump. Quiver. Quiver-quiver. Refusing to take my order to calm down, my left thigh muscle writhes and dances against my clothes.

Distracting at the least, terrifying at the worst, my body tells me that I am not in control. It proclaims, "I will do my own thing, thank you." Thanks. Thanks for what? That I cannot control my muscles that God wired to work when and if I told them to? That I do not know when, where, and how often it will occur? That I do not know if these disruptive movements will become constant, interfere with movements I want to make, become painful, and keep me awake when I want to sleep?

Become disruptive? They already have. Would you want me to take a foreign body our of your eye when you knew my fingers might jump uncontrollably? My former patients didn't want me to, either.

Clamor, peace, annoyance, fright. I have felt them all. Six years ago I feared they meant a yet-worse-than-MS disease. Thank God I don't have to deal with that anymore! For weeks to months at a time I would be only vaguely aware of minor muscle activity. And then the last twenty-four hours. That has been a different story! The ugly "I will do my own thing" has bombarded my brain, interfered with times of rest and awakened me at two-thirty this morning. So what can I do? I can try to deny it happens. Good try. Fat chance that would work! Besides, denial only plunges me into deeper problems.

I can panic. I know. I have. Talk about disruption! Think about it. The impairment disrupts; panic paralyzes. Panic thrusts me into deeper problems yet.

I can ruminate. How long, how much, how frequent? Will it hurt? Will it last the rest of my life? The list of potential questions grows ever longer until my whole universe is stuffed with piles of crumpled paper crammed full with the inquiries.

Or, then, I can drag myself back to the basics. Listen to the psalmist. Wow! What a response to deep trouble:

> *O LORD my God, I take refuge in you; save and deliver me from all who pursue me, or they will tear me like a lion and rip me to pieces with no one to rescue me ... I will give thanks to the LORD because of his righteousness and will sing praise to the name of the LORD Most High.*
> 
> Ps 7:1-2, 17

There is more:

> *I will be glad and rejoice in your love, for you saw my affliction and knew the anguish of my soul.*
> *You have not handed me over to the enemy but have set my feet in a spacious place.*
> *Be merciful to me, O LORD, for I am in distress;*

*my eyes grow weak with sorrow, my soul and my body with grief.*
*My life is consumed by anguish and my years by groaning; my strength fails because of my affliction, and my bones grow weak.*
Ps 31:7-10

And if that is not enough:

*I am in pain and distress; your salvation, O God, protect me.*
*I will praise God's name in song and glorify him with thanksgiving.*
*This will please the LORD more than an ox, more than a bull with its horns and hoofs.*
Ps 69:29-31

The solution is obvious. The process demanding. With God's help I can call it as it really is; praise instead of panic; refuse to be consumed today by tomorrow's possible problems. Thank You, Lord for sharing today the experiences of the psalmist's yesterdays. By Your grace I will overcome!

# Midnight Praise
❧•❧

Listen to Luke tell us the almost-too-much-to-be-true account of Paul and Silas in prison for their faith:

> *After they had been severely flogged, they were thrown into prison, and the jailer was commanded to guard them carefully. Upon receiving such orders, he put them in the inner cell and fastened their feet in the stocks. About midnight Paul and Silas were praying and singing hymns to God, and the other prisoners were listening to them.*
> *Acts 16:23-25*

Singing?<br>
At midnight?<br>
After a flogging?<br>
In the inner cell?<br>
In front of their enemies?

Even as a child, this story wrenched me every time I heard it. Listen to the singing of the whip. Feel the excruciating pain. Experience the weakness from loss of blood.

Did Paul or Silas scream out in pain? Faint? How did they even get into their cell? Paul and Silas had to be spiritual giants. Who else could sing praises to God after such treatment? Certainly I didn't know anyone who I thought could. I knew it was byond my spiritual reach.

But then it was my turn. I was attacked by more than the loss of physical function. All of me was involved. How was I going to function as pastor, physician, husband, parent/grandparent, and friend? I was scared. Really scared! I knew too much. Could I praise God in the middle of this?

Over time the Lord has been teaching me a very special secret. I have learned from the Psalms:

when things get tight, acknowledge your emotions. Tell the Lord how you feel, really feel:

> *Save me, O God, for the waters have come up to my neck. I sink in the miry depths, where there is no foothold. I have come into the deep waters; the floods engulf me. I am worn out calling for help; my throat is parched. My eyes fail, looking for my God.*
>
> *Ps 69:1-3*

And then praise Him. Really praise Him. The deeper the pain, the greater the praise:

> *I will praise God's name in song and glorify him with thanksgiving. This will please the LORD more than an ox, more than a bull with its horns and hoofs.*
>
> *Ps 69: 30-31*

Lord, Your Word shouts the challenge. The psalmists of old set the example. I grasp the concept. My spirit is willing, but I must admit I am skeptical; it doesn't make sense. How can I be thankful when so much has been viciously yanked away. Out of obedience I whisper a faint word of praise. I am somehow strengthened to raise my voice. Cautiously and tentatively I raise my eyes and my voice heavenward. And then I learn— the act of praising puts more praise in my soul. Soon my praise wells up in my soul like an artesian well— no, thrusts upward like a geyser. I hear and feel the praise of the heavenly beings as they raise their voices and as they fall on their faces in adoration.

> Especially I need to praise Him—
> After life has done its worst to me;
> At midnight when I can't sleep;
> In the midst of my adversities.

# Lament and Praise
❖•❖

Listen! You can almost hear his words echo down the centuries as David shouts out his pain (Ps 22).

*My God, my God, why have you forsaken me? Why are you so far from saving me, so far from the words of my groaning?*

v 1

There is more:

*... Trouble is near and there is no one to help ... Roaring lions tearing their prey open their mouths wide against me ... . All my bones are out of joint ... My strength is dried up like a potsherd ... My tongue sticks to the roof of my mouth.*

vv 11, 13-15

The words seem to reverberate one against the other until he has no more strength and they fade into silence.

From the edge of death, he pleads again:

> *But you, O LORD, be not far off; O my Strength, come quickly to help me.*
> *Deliver my life from the sword, my precious life from the power of the dogs.*
> *Rescue me from the mouth of the lions; save me from the horns of the wild oxen.*
>
> vv 19-21

As he cries out to the Lord, praise begins to surge in his spirit:

> *I will declare your name to my brothers; in the congregation I will praise you.*
> *You who fear the LORD, praise him! All you descendants of Jacob, honor him! Revere him, all you descendants of Israel!*
> *For he has not despised or disdained the suffering of the afflicted one; he has not hidden his face from him but has listened to his cry for help.*
> *From you comes the theme of my praise in the great assembly; before those who fear you will I fulfill my vows.*
>
> vv 22-25

And confidence banishes the despair that had nearly destroyed him:

> *The poor will eat and be satisfied; they who seek the LORD will praise him— may your hearts live forever!*
>
> v 26

I identify with David. There have been those kind of days. Pauline, would ask, "Where are you?" And then I would realize I was so preoccupied with my fears and pain that I barred her from my consciousness. I had slammed the door in the face of my greatest human ally. More than that, I had excluded the Lord from my consciousness. In my turmoil, I slammed the door on my Master — the very one who had carried all my load for me. Thank God for His and Pauline's love. They grab my attention, and by God's grace I begin to praise both of them for past benefits. Once again hope banishes fear.

# Pray On
⇥⇤

I really wished I knew the author of Psalm 88. What a story he could tell! For weeks I read, prayed over and discussed this psalm with friends. Its message nearly consumes me. Look on with me. But beware, you may never be the same.

The poet cries out in confidence:

> *O LORD, the God who saves me, day and night I cry out before you. May my prayer come before you; turn your ear to my cry.*
>
> vv 1,2

But then his confidence falters. Instead of answered prayer he visualizes the worst:

> *For my soul is full of trouble and my life draws near the grave.*
> *I am counted among those who go down to the pit; I am like a man without strength.*
>
> vv 3,4

And it is all God's fault:

> *You have put me in the lowest pit ... Your wrath lies heavily upon me ... You have taken from me my closest friends and have made me repulsive to them. I am confined and cannot escape.*
>
> vv 6-8

This is not a new problem. We listen as he reminds God that he has had this problem for a very long time. He seems to be saying, "Why do You not listen? God, can't You remember how long this has been going on?" Listen to his words:

> *But I cry to you for help, O LORD; in the morning my prayer comes before you.*
> *Why, O LORD, do you reject me and hide your face from me? From my youth I have been afflicted and close to death; I have suffered your terrors and am in despair.*
>
> vv 13-15

Confidence has died. Despair reigns. God does not answer. And then in one last convulsion,
he charges God again:

> *You have taken my companions and loved ones from me; the darkness is my closest friend.*
>
> v 18

Consider his plight. For years he has struggled. Endured terrible difficulties. Felt friends' ostracism. Sought God. And all he has is darkness!

Where, I ask, is God? Why doesn't He answer? How much longer must he agonize? Is his problem beyond hope or help? As I wrestle with these questions, the really big ones nearly bowl me over. Could this be my experience some day? Will I suffer in silence even as I agonize before God? What would I do then? Even as I question, the psalmist's words give me direction. Despite the desperate conditions he faced, he continued to pray. When there is nothing else to do, pray on. And on. And on.

And then, I realize that the psalmist failed to do what is so characteristic of these laments— he failed to praise God. Would he have heard God speak if he had praised Him? I don't know. I do know that praise is absolutely vital to faith. I pray, Dear Father, when I am overcome by life's deepest problems, help me to reach out and praise You. Really praise You. Give me that strength if You give me nothing else.

As I pray, the Lord thrusts me forward hundreds of years. The Apostle John makes it ever so bright:

> In *him was life, and that life was the light of men. The light shines in the darkness, and the darkness has not overcome it."*
>
> John 1:5 RSV

Dear Father, I bathe in the Light. May I never fear I will be consumed by darkness.

# Same Ol', Same Ol'

Been there, done that. Over and over, I have read the psalmists' agonizing pleas, listened to their complaints, and watched their stretch of faith and praise to God.

Indulge me. Listen as they confront their issues and their God. Linger and praise with them as they celebrate the resolution.

> *Save me, O God, for the waters have come up to my neck. I sink in the miry depths, where there is no foothold. I have come into the deep waters; the floods engulf me.*
>
> Ps 69:1-2

...

> *I will praise God's name in song and glorify him with thanksgiving. Let heaven and earth praise him, the seas and all that move in them.*
>
> Ps 69:30-34

Or:

*How long, O LORD? Will you forget me forever? How long will you hide your face from me? How long must I wrestle with my thoughts and every day have sorrow in my heart? How long will my enemy triumph over me?*

Ps 13:1-2

...

*But I trust in your unfailing love; my heart rejoices in your salvation. I will sing to the LORD, for he has been good to me.*

Ps 13: 5-6

And then:

*Hear my prayer, O LORD; let my cry for help come to you. My heart is blighted and withered like grass; I forget to eat my food. Because of my loud groaning I am reduced to skin and bones.*

Ps 102:1, 4-5

...

*But you, O LORD, sit enthroned forever; your renown endures through all generations. For the LORD will rebuild Zion and appear in his glory. He will respond to the prayer of the destitute; he will not despise their plea.*

Ps 102:12, 16-17

Over and over, I heard the same pattern. Why couldn't they learn from past experiences? Must they always suffer the pain of their difficulties before they remember to praise the Lord? Won't they ever learn? Just praise Him. I think the Lord would get weary with all this repetition.

Wow! Talk about the pot calling the kettle black! How many times have I replayed the same old script? How long have I suffered before I finally remembered to praise Him? Lord, do You get weary with my repetitions? His answer returns faster than my question approaches His Throne:

> *Come to me, all you who are weary and burdened, and I will give you rest.*
> *Take my yoke upon you and learn from me, for I am gentle and humble in heart, and you will find rest for your souls.*
> Matt 11:28-29

Thank You, Jesus. Help me to come, and come, and come. I want to

> *… continually offer to God a sacrifice of praise— the fruit of lips that confess his name.*
> Heb 13:15

# Yet More; What's Next?
›•‹

**Y**et More. This scene feels like an old rerun. Once again, I hear my doctor describe his findings. And yet it can't be a rerun. It is a different doctor. It's in a different part of my body. This time we are talking about my gut, not muscle strength, not balance. Once again, the news is not good. The MS has taken new prey. We all suspected that. He clarifies the changes; I don't like what I hear. That much change? I could never have guessed. I never felt what he described. And then the reality surges into my brain— I am losing sensation as well as motor function.

**What's Next?**

I am awakened for the second time this morning with panicky feelings. First someone is suffocating. This time it was a child breaking its neck. And then there was, as always, personal application which I find very difficult to shake. I spent time reading God's word, and found great comfort in Hebrews:

*Therefore, since we have a great high priest who*

> has gone through the heavens, Jesus the Son of God, let us hold firmly to the faith we profess. For we do not have a high priest who is unable to sympathize with our weaknesses, but we have one who has been tempted in every way, just as we are— yet was without sin.
>
> Heb 4:14, 15

With that I went back to bed and to sleep. But not for long. I woke up a few minutes later with the devil shouting in my ear, "Who says? How do you know that is true?" And then the fear came. What if I am alone some day and this comes back again?

This morning I am able to get out of bed and read, pray, and write. That may not always be so. Then what? So plausible and so implausible. Can scripture prepare me now for then? Join me as we ponder Psalm 38 and discover how David responded to the threat of progressive disease. The psalmist vividly describes terrible physical problems:

> *I am bowed down and brought very low; all day long I go about mourning.*
> *My back is filled with searing pain; there is no health in my body.*
> *I am feeble and utterly crushed; I groan in anguish of heart.*
>
> Ps 38:6-8

His friends desert him; his enemies poise to attack him:

> *My friends and companions avoid me because of my wounds; my neighbors stay far away.*
> *Those who seek my life set their traps, those who would harm me talk of my ruin; all day long they*

*plot deception.*

Ps 38:11,12

He prays on, and on, and on:

*I wait for you, O LORD; you will answer, O Lord my God.*
*For I said, "Do not let them gloat or exalt themselves over me when my foot slips."*
*For I am about to fall, and my pain is ever with me.*
*I confess my iniquity; I am troubled by my sin.*

Ps 38:15-18

The psalm ends without resolution. Is that all there is? Can I find no solution?

But don't give up yet. There is much more to the story. Quietly Jesus shouted down the corridors of time:

*The Spirit of the Lord is on me, because he has anointed me to preach good news to the poor. He has sent me to proclaim freedom for the prisoners and recovery of sight for the blind, to release the oppressed.*

Luke 4:18.

Hebrews provides the clincher:

*Since the children have flesh and blood, he too shared in their humanity so that by his death he might destroy him who holds the power of death— that is, the devil—and free those who all their lives were held in slavery by their fear of death.*

Heb 2:14,15

My difficulties threaten to blind me to the amazing fact that, no matter what happens in this life, I am assured Jesus has won the battle. Do you hear the deep tones of the old spiritual (that Martin Luther King adopted) "We shall overcome"?

# My Expectation, God's Promise

Five years, nine-and-a-half months ago I heard the fateful pronouncement, "You have MS." The time has rushed and dragged along. There have been good days and bad. But today! Today was a bad, no I mean rotten, putrid, lousy excuse for a day. So what else should I expect? MS has a nasty habit of smashing the best of times. I know that. The memory nauseates me. I shouldn't be surprised at anything it hurls at me. You would think that I'd have gotten this right after so long a time.

I started the day in high expectation. I wanted to write. There were some things I needed to do first. The tasks seemed very manageable. Work a while. Rest awhile. Preserve my energies. And then I could write. That looks great on paper. Any time management expert would pat me on the back, and smile approval. A piece of cake! There is only one problem: MS shouts its disdain at my paper-perfect, time-management-approved plan of action.

My high expectation turned into lower-than-the-gutter realization. Work awhile? My fingers fumbled the pills I was sorting out for next week. Would you believe I needed two rest periods to accomplish that menial task?

As I lay down to rest, memory of the early days spin out of control in my brain. The old fears return. Agitation reigns. Exhausted body; agitated mind. Where, Lord, is the victory of yesterday? Am I sentenced to reruns of former terror? Can I ever get beyond this to a place of persistent, permanent calm?

God, where are You? I have not deserted my commitments to You. You are my King. I stake all of me on the fact of Your faithfulness. You have promised to always be here for me as I need You. Like the Israelites of ancient days, I feel deserted. They had remained faithful to You. Still their enemies crushed them. They scattered in shame leaving their dead behind.

Listen, Lord, to their bitter complaints:

> *But now you have rejected and humbled us; you no longer go out with our armies. You made us retreat before the enemy, and our adversaries have plundered us. You gave us up to be devoured like sheep and have scattered us among the nations. You sold your people for a pittance, gaining nothing from their sale.*
>
> Ps 44:9-12

I push my ears to the ground listening for Your approach. I hear nothing. But, as I listen a stillness comes, my agitation decreases, and then I hear You whispering Your assurance in the words of the old hymn, "How Firm A Foundation."

> Fear not, I am with thee; O be not dismayed,
> For I am thy God, and will still give thee aid;
> I'll strengthen thee, help thee, and cause thee to stand,
> Upheld by My righteous, omnipotent hand.

What's that Lord? Are You saying more?

When through fiery trials thy pathway shall lie,
My grace, all sufficient, shall be thy supply:
The flame shall not hurt thee; I only design
Thy dross to consume and thy gold to refine.

Fiery trials. How fiery? Does my history qualify? Maybe I have only had a dress rehearsal! Your grace. It has been more than adequate to date. I will assume it will continue to be. It is enough. Terrible days may lie ahead. Fatigue and agitation will sometimes drown out Your voice. I know that. But now I can shout my confidence. You will remain faithful to Your covenant. That is enough. And now I can rest.

# What God Has Done
❧•❦

Think. Ponder. Meditate. Reach deeply inside your very spirit. Concentrate on the images your memory projects on the screen of your consciousness. What do you see? What has God done? How has He worked in your life? While you are thinking, allow me to review something of the awesome God I serve.

I try to describe what He does. What word captures the essence of His activity? Power? Creativity? Maybe I need a phrase. Absolute power? Infinite creativity? Not enough? I'll try looking around me. Maybe there I can define what He did.

He spoke. That's it. He spoke. And when He spoke, everything that exists instantly sprang into existence. More than that, everything knelt in obedience to His order. Stars turned on their lights. Volcanos thrust their lava high into the sky. Apple trees blossomed and wafted their fragrance into the crisp air. Red blood cells squeezed through brand new capillaries.

But that is not all. He loved. He loved with all that He is. He still loves. Think of it: He loves every one of us. I mean all six billion of us that are now alive. He loves me

1. Note Sayer's essays touching creativity in *Letters*...

93

with all His power focused into my life. I know He does. I have experienced it.

When I was a child, He put in my heart a desire to know Him. And then he fanned that spark into a flame. When the flame begins to die, He blows over it yet again with the bellows of His Spirit; it explodes from His power.

When I was a young man, God brought Pauline and me together. For forty-five years He has nurtured our relationship. He walks with us through difficult days. He laughs with us in the pleasures of life. He teaches us to imitate His love.

When I started to stumble and "walk like a crab," He came alongside. He crawled with me into the innards of that frightening, cold MRI machine. He wiped away my terrified tears, bolstered my reawakening faith, strengthened my tentative steps, and put a new song in my heart.

My gratitude compels me to shout my praises with the psalmists of old:

*Bless the Lord oh my soul. Bless His holy name.*
103:1

and:

*The Lord lives! Praise be to my Rock! Exalted be God my Savior!*
18:46

and then again:

*Let everything that has breath praise the Lord.*
150:6

I do not know about you, but I cannot help but praise Him.

# No Terror in His Shadow

❖

Contrasting emotions. Terror. Comfort. Contrasting mental pictures. A person with MS who cannot move, can barely speak, and who only sees blurred images. A small bed of daffodil plants that loom brightly out of the early morning darkness, illuminated by our porch lamp. Both of these force themselves into my consciousness.

I read of her in the newspaper yesterday; I knew about her in the remote days when I practiced medicine in this town. Her circumstances strike terror in my heart. Will I share her fate? How long might it take to come about? How long would it last? Could I praise the Lord anyway as she does? What kind of testimony would I give to my community?

The blackness of the night intensifies the beauty of the flowers. The blossoms are more yellow, the leaves more green than ever they were by daylight. That brings comfort to my frightened spirit. The Lord bathes me with the light from His words given to His disciples so many years ago:

> *And why do you worry about clothes? See how the lilies of the field grow. They do not labor or spin. Yet I tell you that not even Solomon in all his splendor was dressed like one of these. If that is how God clothes the grass of the field, which is here today and tomorrow is thrown into the fire, will he not much more clothe you, O you of little faith?*
>
> Matt 6:28-30

Even as I write I experience God's loving care. It replaces the fear of the unknown future that woke me an hour ago. I praise You, my blessed Father. Forgive my tendency to make the maybes of an uncertain future more real than the realities of the certain present. Burn deeply into my spirit the comfort coming from Your Spirit. Bring me closer to You. I need to stay close now to ensure being close then— whenever and however that is. Only to the degree I cling to You can I appropriate the promises given through Your psalmist three thousand years ago:

> *He who dwells in the shelter of the Most High will rest in the shadow of the Almighty. I will say of the LORD, "He is my refuge and my fortress, my God, in whom I trust." Surely he will save you from the fowler's snare and from the deadly pestilence. He will cover you with his feathers, and under his wings you will find refuge; his faithfulness will be your shield and rampart. You will not fear the terror of night, nor the arrow that flies by day.*
>
> Ps 91:1-5a

I recommit myself to dwelling in the shelter; to resting in the shadow. Father, draw me closer.

# Loss Gives Way to Gain
⁕⁓⁕

Gone. Poof. Vanished! Another part of me refuses to function as directed. Once again I look to scripture. What does God say to me in the middle of my loss? What does He say about tears, weeping, anguish? A lot. I printed pages of references, determined to do a thorough search for His message to me— and you.

I heard Him speak in a most unexpected way; from an astonishing psalm.

> *I love the LORD, for he heard my voice; he heard my cry for mercy. Because he turned his ear to me, I will call on him as long as I live. The cords of death entangled me, the anguish of the grave came upon me; I was overcome by trouble and sorrow. Then I called on the name of the LORD: "O LORD, save me!" The LORD is gracious and righteous; our God is full of compassion. The LORD protects the simple hearted; when I was in great need, he saved me. Be at rest once more, O my soul, for the LORD has been good to you. For you, O LORD, have delivered my soul from death,*

*my eyes from tears, my feet from stumbling, that I may walk before the LORD in the land of the living.*

Ps 116:1-9

Hey, Lord, this psalm is not about loss. It is about recovery. That doesn't fit my situation. I can only expect deterioration. Don't You remember?

He spoke to me deep in my spirit. "This psalm *is* about recovery. Maybe not that part of you that you want recovered. But it is about recovery. I grant you peace in the middle of strife, joy in the depths of pain. You can laugh even there. Especially there. More than that, you can rejoin the psalmist and shout out with him:

*O LORD, truly I am your servant; I am your servant, the son of your maidservant; you have freed me from my chains. I will sacrifice a thank offering to you and call on the name of the LORD. I will fulfill my vows to the LORD in the presence of all his people, in the courts of the house of the LORD— in your midst, O Jerusalem. Praise the LORD.*

Ps 116:16-19

Leave it to the Lord. Give Him your loss; He stuffs you with His unending provision. Give Him your tears; He overwhelms you with His eternal joy.

Listen up. Hear my praise echo in the very dungeons of my loss:

*Sing to the LORD a new song; sing to the LORD, all the earth.*
*Sing to the LORD, praise his name; proclaim his salvation day after day.*

*Declare his glory among the nations, his marvelous deeds among all peoples.
For great is the LORD and most worthy of praise.*
                                        Ps 96:1-4a

# My Certainty
❧•❦

*The Lord Jesus is my Great Shepherd. As I follow Him, He shall supply all my needs.*
*I shall graze and rest in the greenest meadows; I shall drink from the choicest quiet streams.*
*He completely refreshes me. He guides me in His paths because He is my shepherd.*
*As I walk through life's darkest valleys— even death itself, You are still with me;*
*guiding, protecting, and comforting. I have no cause for fear.*
*You lay out for me a great feast in the very face of all my difficulties. You anoint me with the oil of Your joy. I am more than satisfied.*
*I know Your goodness and love will pursue me throughout this life and I shall dwell forever in the mansion You have prepared for me.*

Psalm 23 HCH

# PART THREE

# The Lord's Table: Guidelines for Victorious, Productive Living

❖•❖

*I have set you an example that you should do as I have done for you.*

John 13:15

*You did not choose me, but I chose you and appointed you to go and bear fruit— fruit that will last.*

John 15:16

# Introduction: Towels and Branches
❧•❦

Join me in my meditations. Visualize the Celestial Want Ads captivating my attention. Read them with me and watch this advertisement jump off the page.

> Needed: Someone to serve for Me. This position holds no glory. You will be called to serve on short notice. At terribly inconvenient times. Often working alone. You will frequently be doing menial or even unpleasant tasks. Many others will refuse to help. You will get fatigue, sore muscles, thick calluses, and heartache. This job is beyond your likes. Disabled? Impaired? You cannot do this job alone. Let me help— My strength is more than adequate. Disciple, meet me at My Table.
>
> Your Master

•••

Hunkered down in a corner behind a carelessly tossed sandal, I watch as the disciples gather around the table. As I listen, I hear them debate an apparently earth-shattering issue. Who should be washing feet? Ugly job, that. It belongs to a slave. Actually the slave with the least seniority. "Me?," I hear the closest disciple, "Surely not me. I'm not a slave. I am a Disciple of the Master." "I am not the one," another declares." The Master invited me to see Him transfigured. I saw Elijah and Moses!" And so it went around the group. Not me! Surely not me! You've got to be kidding! Do it yourself! And so they sit with grungy feet and grimy attitudes. Each waits for the other to own their inferiority and become the slave.

My eyes are pulled by the quiet swish of cloth. Jesus stands, takes off his tunic, and picks up a towel. I watch in amazement as He pours water into a small basin. What is He up to? Oh, now I get it. Surely He will settle the quarrel; I wonder which disciple He will assign to this job. Yes, I was right. He is walking toward one of His disciples with basin, water, and towel. No! I can't believe my eyes! He does not reach out with authority; He kneels down with love. Tenderly, He picks up the disciple's foot. Splashes it with water. Washes off the grime. Dries the now-clean foot.

You could hear a pin drop. There are no claims of seniority. No glances around the room. No pointed fingers. I do see incredulous stares: guilty expressions; tear-filled eyes. And so Jesus went all the way around the table. He washed the feet of Matthew; Nathaniel; John; Judas, the betrayer; Peter, the firebrand (he first refused then requested his head be washed also); Thomas, the doubter; and all the rest. Never did anyone ask to relieve Him; never did He assign the duty.

The mission complete, Jesus turns to them and speaks with the authority He has as Sovereign Lord of the universe and humble servant of His followers. That authority and love thunder as He speaks:

> *"Do you understand what I have done for you?" he asked them. "You call me 'Teacher' and 'Lord,' and rightly so, for that is what I am. Now that I, your Lord and Teacher, have washed your feet, you also should wash one another's feet. I have set you an example that you should do as I have done for you. I tell you the truth, no servant is greater than his master, nor is a messenger greater than the one who sent him. Now that you know these things, you will be blessed if you do them.*
>
> John 13:12-17

I cannot believe His disciples ever forgot what they saw and felt. Moved beyond their own private emotions, they began to really understand the depths of that great love. They did, I think, come away from that holy event with a new understanding of their roles in the Kingdom of God. Jesus commissioned them. Now it was their turn. Now they are the servants. Now they are to complete the race, cooperating with each other to win the prize. They will always be "about their Father's business." This is not for the idle. Or the fainthearted.

•••

I wonder. What do you think? Did anyone wash Jesus' feet that night?

•••

I understand this command at both the cerebral and gut levels. Throughout all my years as a Christian, I have been challenged to serve; rewarded by my accomplishments; humbled by my failures. I know all of these.

I look across my study to the plaque now sitting in the bookcase. It features a guiding principle of my life. I was given it as a twelve or thirteen-year-old boy: "Camper of the Year." Even now, the message of that plaque is compelling, calling me to action.

> *In all thy ways acknowledge him, and he shall direct thy paths.*
>
> Prov 3:6 KJV

When I was seventeen, my local church gave me an Exhorter's License. I wasn't sure who I was to exhort or what I was to say. I did get the message, "Keep active for the Lord." And so it has always been: "Serve the Lord with gladness." "Work, for the night is coming."

And work I did. As a married college student, I accumulated thirteen (I know, we counted them) positions at the little mission church Polly and I attended. While finishing medical school, I completed my educational and service requirements for ordination. The list goes on and on in many situations over many years. I get tired now counting them. When faced with a challenge, I asked but two questions: Does it need to be done? How will I accomplish it? The final challenge was no exception: practice medicine full time, develop a small group ministry part time. I loved it. The Lord blessed it. Polly was always involved with me in it.

I picked my grass-stained clothes and face off the ground. I was "running" across the church campus when I tripped my lazy foot on a piece of the sidewalk. I needed to get some materials from the church storeroom. Time was of the essence. That fall was but a symbol of coming events. As I told you earlier, I soon had to give up both of my professions. I saw myself as a has-been. I would no longer be able to be active for my Master. I would no longer be able to lead small groups. In the coming months, I considered looking up other Christian has-beens; maybe we could form a self-care group. Maybe I could develop an internet ministry for persons with disabilities. Maybe, maybe, maybe. I tried to develop a prayer support ministry for pastors. I visualized praying for them, learning of their challenges, and praying yet more. I threw out the challenge to some friends and acquaintances in ministry. One responded— once. Again, I struck failure. I was not able to do. I was a cast-off Christian. When I came to myself, I realized that the challenges I had imposed on myself were beyond my fatigue limits. The Lord had graciously intervened and brought these self-imposed challenges to a screeching halt.

Lord, I finally asked, "What do You have in store for me?" His reply: "There is much more for you to learn. I have other insights you need to find. You have been very busy in My service. Now it is time for you to sit and listen. Reflect on my word. I need to move you away from the busyness of life— even the life of ministry you once knew."

...

Reflect. Listen. Receive from the Lord. He has spoken many times over many years. I can confidently anticipate He will speak again. Days, even weeks passed. I only heard silence. And then one day He called out to me. It was as if He sent a special invitation.

> Needed: Someone to bear fruit for me. You must be willing to be pruned. Make no doubt about it, you will be whittled and carved to the point you scarcely will recognize yourself. I

have designs on you that cannot be accomplished unless you first submit to my knife. You will think there is nothing left of you that I can use. Trust Me. Be patient with Me. Howard, meet me in My vineyard.

The Master Gardener

The vineyard? Of course. John 15 has long been a special part of scripture for me. Even as I write, my mind reflects back to my boyhood. I don't remember when I first heard those compelling words:

> *"I am the true vine, and my Father is the gardener. He cuts off every branch in me that bears no fruit, while every branch that does bear fruit he prunes so that it will be even more fruitful."*

John 15:1,2

I don't remember the first sermon I heard on my responsibility to be fruitful for Jesus. I don't remember the first time I heard the gospel song:

> "Nothing but leaves for my Master
> Oh, how His loving heart grieves.
> When, instead of the fruit He is asking,
> I offer Him nothing but leaves."[4]

What a challenge. What a threat! I don't remember where I got the idea: bearing fruit was always about reproducing for Jesus— seeing my friends become Christians. I saw fruit as baskets filled with Saved Souls. I should be able to count them. Talk about a challenging task. How was I to do it? Where should I begin? Forget that I was shy about my faith in my everyday world. The years passed. I came to realize that doing other stuff for Jesus also counted as part of the harvest. That was easier. I could always pick up another project for the Kingdom.

And so, I vacillated from excitement to discouragement. My faith required I keep busy in the heavenly vineyard. Over the years, the Lord blessed my ministry for Him. I saw fruit; rarely it was seeing a friend come to Christ. More often it was teaching and encouraging those already in the vineyard with me.

Talk about a heavenly High! For two long weekends, I trained twenty people in the techniques of small group leadership. Within three months, forty percent of the small congregation was involved in small groups. I envisioned baskets and baskets of fruit!

And then (you remember well), I crashed. For weeks the Lord patiently worked with me over issues of loss and fear. And then He moved me back to John 15. This time His word shouted a truth I had long overlooked.

*Remain in me, and I will remain in you. No branch can bear fruit by itself; it must remain in the vine. Neither can you bear fruit unless you remain in me. I am the vine; you are the branches. If a man remains in me and I in him, he will bear much fruit; apart from me you can do nothing ... If you remain in me and my words remain in you, ask whatever you wish, and it will be given you. This is to my Father's glory, that you bear much fruit, showing yourselves to be my disciples ... You did not choose me, but I chose you and appointed you to go and bear fruit—fruit that will last.*
                                    John 15: 4,5,7,8,16

I haven't the faintest clue about how many times I have meditated on this passage. But this time the passage exploded with the Holy Spirit's enlightenment. Wow! What truth He confided to me. Bearing fruit for Jesus is not about what I do for Him. It is about what He does in and through me. It is about what happens when I am intimately joined with Him. My task is to expectantly saturate myself with His presence. When I do that, He reproduces Himself in me. Then I cannot help but be fruitful for Him. Grab this insight: He promises fruit coming from the vine— Himself. Permanent fruit. He tells me to ask Him; He will provide what I need to be yet more productive. He cuts away all that I have done in my own power. He strips away the superfluous. I don't want to tell you what all He has and is trimming away from me. I won't ask what He wants to do with you.

God's great truths often come in packages. For seven years now He has been teaching me. My Master shouts from His word; He instructs from my life experiences, "Serve for me. Sacrifice yourself for others in my name. Don't try to produce fruit— you will fall on your face. Abide in me— reside ever more closely. You will produce fruit— I guarantee it."

Some days I seem almost like I used to be. Most of the time I can do only a little. And then there are <u>those</u> days, days when I can hardly pick up a towel. Forget the basin. Forget the water. When that happens, I frequently start worrying about my productivity as a Christian. When I abide in Him, there is more peace. I don't have to prove anything. He abides in me, and, abiding, He somehow turns my major limitations into His opportunities. I don't even have to measure the harvest!

During these extraordinary seven years, my Master has been teaching me many things about being His disciple. I am learning more and more about the responsibilities and privileges of being His servant. I am totally persuaded that my disabilities do not deprive me of even one benefit of discipleship. Likewise they do not release me from any of the responsibilities of being a child of God. I have learned a lot. I have so much more to learn.

I am learning a new way to walk. I have taken numerous falls. The Lord is teaching me perseverance. Better balance. More graceful falls.

Walk with me. Relive your own journey. Your own struggles. Anticipate your own progress. Together we can each become more nearly conformed to Jesus' image.

# Meditations

# The Gauntlet

So what's a person to do? I have lots of ideas but no place to use them. Lots of desire to minister but no one to minister to. I'm a used-to-be, you'll remember. It's Sunday afternoon; I am alone with my thoughts. Polly is out doing her ministry. She has the opportunity to sing. She has the audience to sing to. She has the skills. It's enough to make a grown man cry. Do my tears come from a sense of loss or from an attitude of self-pity?

I hear the key in the door, her steps in the hallway. She walks like that only when she is excited. I will soon get a report. What can she share that will shake my gloom? And share she does! The audience obviously appreciated her music; some sang or hummed along with her. Some in the audience listened intently to the message and nodded in agreement. The minister's devotion so captivated Polly that she brought a copy of his outline. "You'll want to read this," she said.

Her enthusiasm drags me from my melancholy; snaps me to full attention. I understand the response to her singing. Everyone responds to her like that— even when they are in their mid-eighties and confined to wheelchairs. I don't understand the enthusiasm over the meditation. Old brains continue to respond to favorite music of yesteryear. It is quite something else for them to absorb the concepts of a fresh meditation. That is, unless the minister speaks their language, identifies with their concerns, and challenges them to relevant response.

At eighty-five, Rev. Elmer Boileau is older than some of them. He throws them the gauntlet. Their lives are not yet over. There is much they can do in service to God and others. Listen to his suggestions. Any of them can pray and praise God. They can smile when they talk with others. They can say, "I love you." They can thank the nurses and kitchen staff. They can listen to someone who has a heartache. They can share with others. No wonder Polly is excited!

Pastor Boileau, your words convict me. I'm not even sixty-five yet. I live in my own home; drive my own car (sometimes, anyway); interact with friends and neighbors. And I called myself a "has been?"

Polly, your enthusiasm is contagious. There is a ministry for me. Rejoice with me as I search for it. Engage with me as I enter into it.

Walk with me. Relive your own journey. Together we can each become more nearly conformed to Jesus' image.

# Grow with Me
❧•❧

How can I describe the awesome beauty I see through my study's sliding glass door? Think of the multi-hued greens. Imagine the wide range of browns from the palest russet to the deepest chocolate. Concentrate on the soft focus in the far distance and the sharply defined edges of the closest objects. In your mind, experience the velvety soft and the stubbornly sharp objects. Imagine how the scene changes from the foggy early morning as the sun begins to shine on the marsh in the distance to the glaring mid-afternoon pools of light and shadow formed by nearby oak trees.

Trying as hard as I can, I can only give you a vague notion. At best, I can only hint at the images that burn indelibly in my brain, that stir my deepest emotions. You can turn impressions into reality only by sitting along side me and experiencing the landscape for yourself. You come to my door with basic ideas; you leave my study with personal experience.

My life is like that. For many years I have followed my Jesus. I have learned, grown, struggled, rejoiced, triumphed, and failed. My reality of today is only the mist of tomorrow.

As challenging and rewarding my adventures with Christ have been, they fail to define the rigors and rewards of discipleship that are to come. How will Christ use my weaknesses to evidence His strength? How can my limited energy be maximized by His awesome resources? What fruit will I bear as I abide in Him? How will my testimony of His presence in my life impact the lives of others? How much more of my Savior will I experience and understand? I don't know; I resolve to find out.

God's Word clearly instructs me in the testimony of St. Paul:

> *However, as it is written: "No eye has seen, no ear has heard, no mind has conceived what God has prepared for those who love him" ... We have not received the spirit of the world but the Spirit who is from God, that we may understand what God has freely given us.*
> 
> 2 Cor 2: 9, 12

Listen! Christ speaks in the paraphrase of a famous poet:

> *"Come, grow with me.*
> *My best is yet to be.*
> *Eternity.*
> *For which the now is made."*

Join me in the adventure!

# Choices
⇒•⇐

We turned on the VCR and snuggled into our green La-Z-Boy recliners. We anticipated a lighthearted romance[5]. We got a tear-jerking account of Garret Blake, trapped between what had been and what could be. Listen with us as we learn about his wife Catherine's death. Hear the agony in his voice. Watch with us as we view the shrine he set up in her memory. See how that special place took over all of his life. Everything had changed. Catherine died; he gave up his dream to build boats. Everything remained the same. Garret refused to let anything about her go. Feel the tension build as his father, Dodge, lived all of this with him. At last he had all he could take. With deadly accuracy he told Garret his options, "You choose— the past or the future. Pick one and stick with it." Like a wild animal caught in a corner, Garret lashed out at his father's insensitivity. How dare he upset his carefully defended memories!

Skillful acting. Beautiful scenery. Challenging plot. I got all of that— and more. For days I ruminated on Garret's decision. I thrust my history into his. What had I done— protected myself remembering the way things were, or challenged myself reaching out into the ways things might become?

I look to the Apostle Paul for help. He contrasts his past with his present. He had a lot to remember. Listen to his history:

*If anyone else thinks he has reasons to put confidence in the flesh, I have more: circumcised on the eighth day, of the people of Israel, of the tribe of Benjamin, a Hebrew of Hebrews; in regard to the law, a Pharisee; as for zeal, persecuting the church; as for legalistic righteousness, faultless.*

Phil 3:4-6

History adds to that list. Paul was a member of the Sanhedrin. This body was composed of only seventy members out of all of the Hebrew nation. Talk about power, it had it all— legislative, executive, judicial! Listen to his present:

*But whatever was to my profit I now consider loss for the sake of Christ. What is more, I consider everything a loss compared to the surpassing greatness of knowing Christ Jesus my Lord, for whose sake I have lost all things. I consider them rubbish, that I may gain Christ and be found in him ... I want to know Christ and the power of his resurrection and the fellowship of sharing in his sufferings, becoming like him in his death, and so, somehow, to attain to the resurrection from the dead.*

Phil 3:7-11

My history is somewhat like Garret's. I didn't choose to have MS any more than he chose to be a widower. Like Garret, I had to make a choice of living in the past or reaching out into the future. It is not a choice made once and then forgotten. I have to choose over and over again. Frequently. Perhaps daily. I get sick from hearing myself say, "I will not live in the past."

Sometimes I longingly remember the old days. My determination sometimes wavers. Then the Lord helps me join Paul:

> *Not that I have already obtained all this, or have already been made perfect, but I press on to take hold of that for which Christ Jesus took hold of me. Brothers, I do not consider myself yet to have taken hold of it. But one thing I do: Forgetting what is behind and straining toward what is ahead, I press on toward the goal to win the prize for which God has called me heavenward in Christ Jesus.*
>
> Phil 3:12-14

Empowered by the Holy Spirit I recommit myself to that goal and wheel into my future.

# The Garden

Alone. Two sprouts. Five leaves. Surrounded by nothing but hardwood mulch, the isolated iris plant reaches heavenward on a spring morning. Last year it was part of a mature bed of other irises. For years, it and its companions, did what irises do best— developed beautiful blossoms, wafted delicate scents into our garden and reproduced themselves. Predictably. Quietly. Without fanfare.

But then our landscaper attacked with sharp shovel and heavy hand. The entire bed had to be thinned out. We determined to move them all. New location. New vigor. New opportunity. But one was left behind.

My life is sometimes ugly like that. Sharp shovels. Heavy hands. Massive disruption. Isolation. My life is sometimes challenging like that. New location. New opportunities. New paradigm. Will I make it a new opportunity? Will I find new vigor?

Irises don't have memories, but I do. How was it for me before my disruption? Did I reach heavenward? Produce beautiful blossoms? Sweeten the air? Are lives different today because of my actions then? Did my love for Jesus make a difference in someone's life? My days were overcast— senses disrupted; memory confused. Lord, I pled, I need Your special blessing. And bless me He did as He brought two special friends who shared how God had used me in their spiritual development. My need; His response! I'm glad I'm not an iris!

Irises don't reflect, but I do. Sometimes I feel so isolated. I can't see any blossom; smell any perfume. I long to be part of the old bed. Together we had flung God's fragrance into a putrid world. Dejected, forlorn, heavy-hearted I turned to God's Word and discovered a kindred spirit (Psalm 42). He was downcast

His tears were his only food. His bones suffered mortal agony. He used to lead the procession into the Temple; now he can't go and meet his God. How awful!

Misery loves company. Who better can I cry with? Who else knows the depth of my distress? The psalmist and I can have a wonderful pity-party! What empathy! What stories we can relate! There is only one problem: he won't cooperate. He has another agenda; another solution. Listen as he concludes the psalm:

> *Why are you downcast, O my soul?*
> *Why so disturbed within me?*
> *Put your hope in God,*
> *for I will yet praise him,*
> *my Savior and my God.*
>
> v 11

One life. His garden. My opportunity. Grow. Blossom. Perfume the air. Reproduce. By faith I assert I am planted where He knows I can best serve Him now. Sometimes lonely for the old days of ministry? Yes. Isolated from His presence? Never.

# My Lystra
❧•❦

You've got to be kidding! How can I believe that? If it weren't in scripture I would just laugh. But it is in scripture. Luke was dead serious when he related a day in the ministry of the Apostle Paul as recorded in Acts 14. If he had been a journalist, he could have submitted the following stories to the local newspaper:

**Stranger Comes to Town, Heals Local Cripple**
**Paul and Barnabas Refuse to be Called Gods**
**Jealous Jews Incite Riot, Stone Paul.**

Each story details the important facts. The congenital cripple sprang from his squat and walked without any lessons. They cried of Paul, "He is Zeus." The local priest hastened to bring animals for sacrifice. Paul and Barnabas struggled to restrain their heathen ecstacy. Jealous Jews from previous towns incited a riot, stoned Paul, and then to forever get rid of this obnoxious Christian, dragged him out of the city thinking he was just a corpse.

But that is not the end of the story; the best part would

never be accepted by the local editor. Let scripture speak for itself.

> *But after the disciples had gathered around him, he got up and went back into the city. The next day he and Barnabas left for Derbe. They preached the good news in that city and won a large number of disciples. Then they returned to Lystra ... strengthening the disciples and encouraging them to remain true to the faith. "We must go through many hardships to enter the kingdom of God," they said.*
> Acts 14:20-22

It's as if Paul declared, "It is all just part of a day's discipleship."

All in a day's discipleship? Only rarely have I been excluded because I am a Christian. I have never felt the impact of a stone hurled at me. When did I last struggle to my feet; lean on the arms of fellow Christians; hurry on to the next town to tell my spiritual story; return to the people who wanted to terminate me?

Lord, I'm not asking for death struggles, but I do want to learn from Paul's experience. I determine to *"throw off everything that hinders and the sin that so easily entangles ... and run with perseverance the race marked out for [me]."* Heb 12:1.

Where will the Lord take me? What difficulties will I encounter? What opportunities will I have to bear fruit for Jesus? I don't know. He does. That is enough.

How will the Lord work in your journey? Where will He take you? What will it cost? What of His mercy will you experience. Trust Him. He has a gracious plan. Just for you.

# On Beard and Keyboard

Shave that beard. Don't forget to floss. Stretch those muscles before you finish dressing. Put the dirty dishes in the dishwasher. Check your e-mail. It's time to rest. The list goes on and on. The list shows up again every morning. I get tired from doing all those necessary things. I wish I had more energy for the pleasures of my life: family times, friendships, prayer, Bible study, preparation for small group, and my writing.

I get tired of doing them. I find I am sometimes ungrateful and find it hard to be thankful for what my master does for me. I sometimes forget to ask his special strength for the day. I often forget promises of scripture:

> *Praise the LORD, O my soul,*
> *and forget not all his benefits ...*
> *who satisfies your desires with good things*
> *so that your youth is renewed like the eagle's.*
> Ps 103:2,5

and

> *... but those who hope in the LORD*
> *will renew their strength.*
> *They will soar on wings like eagles;*
> *they will run and not grow weary,*
> *they will walk and not be faint.*
>
> Isa 40:31

I don't have it hard. Not really. Think of John the Baptist. Watch him as he invades the wild bees' nest to gather honey for his Spartan diet. He didn't even have a convenience store to get bread, or for that matter, Caladryl® to treat his bee stings!

The Apostle Paul puts me to shame. I stagger at his life of disciplined service to the Lord Jesus. Think of it— He taught, encouraged, and disciplined many Christians while shackled to Roman guards. Did rats run through his cell and interrupt his thoughts? Did he ever get any diversionary recreation time in the prison courtyard? Did he have enough vitamins in his diet? I don't know about those things, but I do know we have much of the New Testament because of his faithful service.

The Lord will not let me off the hook. The scripture pounds in my ears as the writer of Hebrews shouts the Lord's urgent appeal:

> *Therefore, since we are surrounded by such a great cloud of witnesses, let us throw off everything that hinders and the sin that so easily entangles, and let us run with perseverance the race marked out for us. Let us fix our eyes on Jesus, the author and perfecter of our faith, who for the joy set before him endured the cross, scorning its shame, and sat down at the right*

*hand of the throne of God. Consider him who endured such opposition from sinful men, so that you will not grow weary and lose heart.*
Hebrews 12:1-3

The Lord speaks, too, through the encouraging words of dear friends who wrote,

"Howard, we thank God for you and your ministry... Our prayer is that our Lord hold you very close, and may His Spirit refresh your spirit. We pray a special touch for healing. We love you and we will pray daily for you. Bob and Evie."

What a God! What an example! What friends! What else could I need?

Time to get up! Stretch! Where's the phone? Today is our daughter's birthday. Keyboard, here I come. My manuscript is waiting.

# On Vines and Fish
❧•❦

Promise, promise, promise. Covenant. Assurance. And that's not all. Lots. Much. Overflowing. Gobs. And still there is more. Permanent.

Lord, I have to take You at face value on this one. I don't think there is any way I can pull it off. I have been up long enough today to change the pillow cases. It's bed-change day; fixing the pillows is my job, and I am ready for a long rest. Tomorrow is small group; I need to finish preparation. We haven't met for three weeks. We have a new couple joining us. There is no way I want to cancel.

Do You remember what You promised? Of course You do.

> *"I am the vine, and you are the branches. Whoever remains in me, and I in him, will bear much fruit ... If you remain in me and my words remain in you, then you will ask for anything you wish, and you shall have it ... My Father's glory is shown by your bearing much fruit; and in this way you become my disciples.*

*... You did not choose me; I chose you and appointed you to go and bear much fruit, the kind of fruit that endures."*
John 15:5,7,8,16 TEV

My corner of the vineyard is really very small. There is the small group I lead and there is my writing. The rest (what little there is of it) is the day-to-day stuff of normal relationships. A few scrawny grapes. Half dried. On their way to becoming raisins. What more do I have to offer? And I am not off to a good start for the week on this one. If I am to have even a small harvest, I need maximum help.

What's that You say, Lord? Oh, You mean the little guy's lunch— five small loaves of bread and two dinky fish. He had carried them all day. Doubtless his lunch sack had been smushed long ago. Yuck! Five squished rolls. Two smelly fish. Five thousand very hungry people— and the Lord. John 6: 9-12

Time passes; the sun will soon set. Watch with me; five thousand very satisfied men (plus all the women and kids) are on their way home. Twelve very tired disciples are still filling twelve borrowed baskets with the leftovers from the feast. I wonder— what did the little kid think? Imagine how big his eyes got when he watched that huge banquet spring from his shabby lunch.

Lord, look at my eyes. Are they dilated from astonishment at what You propose to do in my life? The boy offered his fish. I offer my exhaustion. That's all I have today. I'm glad You have Your-sized plans for my life. I'm glad You can pull it off!

# Pleasant Places
⇶•⇷

Disappointed again! I just got home from the doctor's office. I learned that there is no medication or other treatment that will give me even a little better function. I knew I was taking the right medications; doing the right things. I must admit, though, I hoped my doctor could make an adjustment or two that would give a little improvement. But no, that is not to be. Reality struck again!

I lay down to rest; I was really tired from the long wait and the intensity of the interchange with the doctor. As I lay there, I became aware that the world was closing in. I thought of cramped quarters, tight places, inability to move about freely. I remembered friends of other times and other places. They are no longer available to me. As I thought, I again felt squeezed. It doesn't take much insight to realize that I was feeling loss. Feeling alone.

And then the Lord spoke to me. I thought of the psalm's promise:

> *LORD, you have assigned me my portion and my cup;*
> *you have made my lot secure.*

*The boundary lines have fallen for me in pleasant places;*
*surely I have a delightful inheritance.*
*You have made known to me the path of life;*
*you will fill me with joy in your presence,*
*with eternal pleasures at your right hand.*
Ps 16: 5-6,11

Listen as the Lord whispers in my ears, "You are not restricted. My joy is yours. To me there are no crowded spaces. What I have I give to you."

Reaching across the centuries, Nehemiah's exhortation to his people burned deeply into my spirit:

*"Go and enjoy choice food and sweet drinks, and send some to those who have nothing prepared. This day is sacred to our Lord. Do not grieve, for the joy of the LORD is your strength."*
Neh 8:10

Warm, fuzzy feelings. Serenity. Comfort. Strength. Once again the Lord met my need.

"Listen up," the Lord said, "There is much more to Nehemiah's directive. Look at that passage again." I looked. *"Send some to those who have nothing prepared,"* the passage declared. The serenity faded. In its place, the Lord threw out the challenge, "My blessings are not for you alone. I gave to you so you might give to others. Think big. Reflect with My servant, Paul,

*'Praise be to the God and Father of our Lord Jesus Christ, the Father of compassion and the God of all comfort, who comforts us in all our troubles, so that we can comfort those in any*

*trouble with the comfort we ourselves have received from God.'"*

2 Cor 1:3-4

Pleasant places. God's comfort for me that meets all my needs— even in the face of functional loss. God's comfort from me to someone who feels constricted, desperate, or alone.

Accept the challenge with me. What place is there for disappointment?

# Stretching

Our pastor[6] talks to us about walking our faith. We walk day in, day out. Month in, month out. We are in it for the long journey

The Apostle Paul talks to me about running the race; about stretching to reach the goal.

My body talks to me about spastic muscles— muscles made tight by the MS. I last ran seven years ago; I can walk only very short distances and that with help.

I hate tight muscles. The tighter they are, the harder it is to move The harder it is to move, the more tired I get. The more tired I get, the harder and more fatiguing it is to stretch those taut muscles.

I have a choice— stretch or lose muscular function. Stretch or get progressively more tired. The choice is up to me.

You better believe I stretch. Carefully. Completely. On schedule. And as I stretch I remember I will get less and less benefit from those very exercises. That doesn't hamper my dedication; I intend to persevere!

MS dictates progressive loss; my faith offers progressive gain. Day after day I can exercise my spirit. Week after week I have more opportunity to run the race with Jesus. Month after month I can stretch out toward the goal of becoming more and more like my savior. More exercise produces more faith. More faith stimulates more obedience. More obedience yields more fruit for Jesus. More and more and more!

I have a choice— Become more like Jesus or gradually lose the ability to run my spiritual race. I choose to make Paul's commitment my own:

> *I want to know Christ and the power of his resurrection and the fellowship of sharing in his sufferings, becoming like him in his death, and so, somehow, to attain to the resurrection from the dead. Not that I have already obtained all this, or have already been made perfect, but I press on to take hold of that for which Christ Jesus took hold of me ... I do not consider myself yet to have taken hold of it. But one thing I do: Forgetting what is behind and straining* (stretching [ASV]) *toward what is ahead, I press on toward the goal to win the prize for which God has called me heavenward in Christ Jesus.*
> Phil 3:10-14

I choose to walk. Run. Stretch out to the goal.

# Compulsing
⇾•⇽

"Howard, stop talking! I asked a simple question. You gave me one of your more-than-I-will-ever-want-to-know answers. You are compulsing again."

"Compulsing" is our home-grown word; germinated in the soil of verbal necessity. It describes my sometimes behavior. Compulsive. Driven. Agitated. Churned. Sometimes even those aren't enough words!

Me? Compulsive?

Ask my mother. "You have the wrong Howard." she replies. "This call got misdirected by the Celestial PBX. That is not my son! Visionary, yes. Out of control, no."

Ask Polly. "I think he has metamorphosed. His take-it-as-it-comes acceptance sometimes drove me up a wall. But today? We really do need all those words."

Why me? Why now? For weeks I sought the answer. Twitching muscles, crawling skin, disrupted sleep, queasy stomach, and more yelled out my loss of control. Did I do it to myself? Was I studying too hard; resting too little; failing to recreate?

I was intense. To better know Jesus. Better show his love in all my relationships. I had a zillion questions. The more

I questioned, the more intense I got. I felt isolated. Alone. Discipleship became drudgery.

In the middle of this nightmare, the Lord led me back some twenty-five hundred years. The returned exiles have finished rebuilding the walls of Jerusalem. It is time they concentrate on spiritual matters. Ezra and Nehemiah called them all together and for half a day read and explained the law to them. As I read, the Lord grabbed my attention. Listen with me to their next words:

> *Then Nehemiah the governor, Ezra the priest and scribe, and the Levites who were instructing the people said to them all, "This day is sacred to the LORD your God. Do not mourn or weep." For all the people had been weeping as they listened to the words of the Law. Nehemiah said, "Go and enjoy choice food and sweet drinks, and send some to those who have nothing prepared. This day is sacred to our Lord. Do not grieve, for the joy of the LORD is your strength."*
>
> Neh 8:9-10

Where was my joy, my strength?

But maybe I wasn't doing it to myself. Maybe there was a better answer. And then I remembered conversations with patients years ago. "Remember," I would say, "MS can do anything." Was it doing that to me now? Was this really a medical issue? And so I called my neurologist. She listened to my story. I could hear her smile over the phone. "I think we need to make some adjustments in your treatment."

Voila! I sleep better now. Food sits easier in my stomach. I'm more connected with others. Joy is returning. I was seeing Jesus as a cowboy driving me heavenward; now I sometimes feel the gentle nudge of the Shepherd's staff as he directs and leads me.

We are still fiddling with my medical regimen. I still have a zillion questions about my faith. With God's help, I can confidently expect further improvement— physically and spiritually.

By faith I can proclaim the Lord is my joy and my strength.

And I won't forget my medicine.

# The Parable of the Horse

The kingdom of heaven is like a horse named Pilgrim and a cowboy named Tom. Pilgrim is a horse with a terrible past and a tortured present. The cowboy knows horses as few people do.

Yesterday, Pauline and I saw the movie, "The Horse Whisperer"[7]. In the theater of your mind join the two of us as we relive this tale. Look on in horror as Pilgrim and his rider are terribly injured. It is as if the whole world crashes into them. The horse really should have been destroyed; the owner refused. Eventually Pilgrim's body healed but his spirit did not. He had been a well trained riding horse. Valuable to his owner. Now he thrashes wildly in his stall. See the anger and the fear contort his face. No one can control him; you enter the stall at your own risk.

But then Pilgrim meets Tom. What a meeting! Not only does he know horses, he seems to talk a common language with them. His friends call him, "The Horse Whisperer." Patiently he communicates with Pilgrim, always advancing toward the goal of the horse maximizing his potential. In my heart I ask if Pilgrim will ever change. How long will it take? Hear Tom's reply, "That all depends on Pilgrim."

I, like Pilgrim, have a terrible past. The Lord forgave that when, fifty-two years ago, I confessed my sin and invited Him into my life. Since then He has been working in and on me. How much will I change? How long will it take? That depends on me.

I, too have crashed. Five years ago, my whole world caved in. I felt tortured, discarded. My future seemed utterly stripped of potential. But then, my Lord spoke. Patiently. Persistently. Persuasively. He continues to speak, sometimes so quietly I have to really concentrate to hear Him. Sometimes His voice thunders. I would have to stuff my ears with the cotton of indifference to not hear Him.

How much will my spirt heal? How long will it take? Will I be of value to His kingdom? That all depends on me. The Lord has done and continues to do His part. Paul's prayer penetrates deeply into my soul:

> *I pray that out of his glorious riches he may strengthen you with power through his Spirit in your inner being, so that Christ may dwell in your hearts through faith. And I pray that you, being rooted and established in love, may have power, together with all the saints, to grasp how wide and long and high and deep is the love of Christ, and to know this love that surpasses knowledge— that you may be filled to the measure of all the fullness of God.*
>
> Eph 3:16-19

# How Then Shall I Live?
❧•❦

Ten Steps? Did I hear right? Wow, that really cramps my style! In one short paragraph, my neurologist reshaped how I am to live. She knows my muscle endurance is quite limited. She knows I am at risk for a nasty fall. She doesn't want that to happen, so she lays down her edict— anytime I walk more that ten steps I am to use a walker.

Now, in a general sense, I am in favor of walkers. How many times had I ordered them for my patients? I'd hate to guess. But in specific terms, I hate the whole idea. It's really not that serious is it? (Psst— don't tell anybody, but I really know in my head that it is that serious). Walkers are terribly restrictive. I can hear a physical therapist lay down the rule, "Keep both of your hands on the walker." How can I carry anything when I walk? So how am I to do one of my major household tasks— setting the table?

Whittle. Chip. Gouge. So what's next? Some day I'll live in a wheel chair rather than just use one part time. Some day I may need help rolling over in bed. Some day— I don't know what. I don't know when. I do know it is downhill from here. That is the nature of progressive disease. Indeed, that is the nature of human kind. We are all downhill from here. Listen to the psalmist remind us

> *As for man, his days are like grass,*
> *he flourishes like a flower of the field;*
> *the wind blows over it and it is gone,*
> *and its place remembers it no more.*
>
> Ps 103:15-16

But not all downhill. Other words come to mind. Browse the New Testament with me. Feast your eyes on these delicacies:

Conformed

> *... whom ... he also predestined to be conformed to the likeness of his Son,*
>
> Rom 8:29

Reaching

> *... we shall become mature people, reaching to the very height of Christ's full stature.*
>
> Eph 4:13 TEV

Transformed
> *... but be transformed by the renewing of your mind.*
>
> Rom 12:2

Knit

> *... That their hearts might be comforted, being knit together in love.*
>
> Col 2:2 KJV

Downhill? Not on your life! I am called to become more and more like my Master. There is no limit. For the rest of my life, I can grow as His disciple. By God's grace, I am on my way toward the summit.

# The List

Aha! What a wonderful night's sleep! Oh, how good that feels. I'm refreshed. It's Sunday; we go to church and then I want to write a meditation this afternoon.

Devastated. Devoured. Overwhelming Fatigue, my nemesis, you strike again. And with a vengeance. I have shaved, bathed, and brushed my teeth. I have put on my shirt, pants, and stockings. Big job! And now I sit resting my forearms on my thighs— too fatigued to finish dressing.

The psalmist talked about going with the multitude to the temple, singing and shouting as he led the people (Ps 42). I think about trying to get enough energy to finish dressing, walk down the hall, get in the car, and ride to the church.

Whew, I'm home from church. I made it! And now I'll rest until lunch. Lunch is over; I've slept an hour and a half; I'm ready to try again.

Lord, I want to talk about my quiet times with You. They vary so much. Sometimes I listen, we talk, I pray; then I go on with the other events of my day. Some times I listen to You as I read Your word. The time is, well, heavenly. There is so much to hear; so much to learn; so many adjustments

I need to make so I can be more conformed to Your image. Frankly, Lord, it sometimes wears me out. I look at my prayer list. There are so many to pray for. Polly. Our children/ grandchildren; all with special needs. Unsaved friends. Others who are very ill. My small group currently scattered for winter-escape from the snows of the north. Colleagues in ministry. The list goes on. Just look at it, Lord. So much to pray for. It's too much for me to handle today.

His quiet assurance thunders in my ears. "My, son, I'll take the list for you today. Do you forget the words I had Paul say to you?

> *'And in the same way-by our faith —the Holy Spirit helps us with our daily problems and in our praying. For we don't even know what we should pray for nor how to pray as we should, but the Holy Spirit prays for us with such feeling that it cannot be expressed in words. And the Father who knows all hearts knows, of course, what the Spirit is saying as he pleads for us in harmony with God's own will.'*
> 
> *Rom 8:26-27* TLB

Go now. Take a long rest. There are things for you to do tomorrow that I do not do. Remember those bills you need to pay?"

# Being There

I woke with a start. Disquiet. Uneasiness. Something is wrong! Slipping into my best diagnostic mode, I start to check out the possibilities. Chipmunk or mouse gnawing in the wall? Nope. Thunder clapping? Not a chance. Do I hurt, am I able to move okay? The questions continue. The answers only lead to more questions.

And then my lightbulb flashes on! "Blessed are they that mourn for they shall be comforted" (Matt 5:4). Before my anxiety rubs off on you, let me clue you in.

Our Tuesday afternoon small group is studying the Beatitudes. Picture me getting ready to lead the group. I'm deep in thought. I look up "mourn" in my various study aids. I visualize a special friend who recently buried his wife after more than 60 years of sharing life's joys and pains. I think of the special concerns within our group. I pray for the session.

Slip forward a few days. Small group has just concluded. We pondered Jesus' meaning. I mentioned the special friend; we prayed God's comfort engulf him. We mourned together for the single mother staggering under her load. Major illness. Broken furnace. Coming winter. On a scale of 1-7 we had an

8+ successful session. Good group. Wonderful, concerned members.

So what's the big deal? Why the sleep-shattering experience? It hit me broadside— throughout that whole experience I never thought about Polly's pain of the past seven years. I never considered my own losses. They are there. For sure. We can't do the things we used to do. Visualize with me. I sit in my power wheelchair looking out through my study's sliding glass door. Polly is putting her garden to sleep for the winter. She gets cold; I stay warm. She gets tired; I take a nap. Gardening is her special joy— joy mixed with battles over beetles and weeds. My heart thrills with her joy. My heart aches that I can't help jerk the weeds, smash the bugs, carry in produce. The days of doing those kinds of things together are irrevocably past.

I pondered mourning. I led discussion about people in pain experiencing deep loss. It didn't remind me of our losses. That's good. I cannot live in the valley of despair. But then that's terribly bad. I deprived both of us from once again experiencing God's comfort. It stole from me the opportunity to comfort the most important person in my life. In short, I lost the opportunity to faithfully follow my Lord. I completely ignored the Lord's message to me through Paul:

> *Praise be to the God and Father of our Lord Jesus Christ, the Father of compassion and the God of all comfort, who comforts us in all our troubles, so that we can comfort those in any trouble with the comfort we ourselves have received from God. For just as the sufferings of Christ flow over into our lives, so also through Christ our comfort overflows.*
> 2 Cor 1:3-5

That's what shattered my sleep this morning.

That's what must organize my day today. My time of personal devotions await me. There are bills to pay. I have a friend I want to e-mail. Those I can and will do. Those, if you will, are clusters of activity. My biggest opportunity is to "be there" for my bride of forty-six years.

Stuff me full with your comfort, Lord. I acknowledge how much I need it. Overwhelm me with the desire to flood my sweetheart with Your comfort that just now saturates me. I acknowledge I have not been sensitive enough. Comforting enough. Enough like You.

# The Long Road Back

In April, 1993 I sat in the ashes of my burned-out dual careers scraping my sores with the potsherd of broken dreams. I hurt. I felt alone. Afraid. Bewildered. How could I be of any help to anybody? What was going to happen to me? My clinical left brain cast frightening images of what MS would probably do to me. My pastoral right brain struggled to find any vision of how God could use me.

But God was not through with me. Faithfully He worked. Patiently He revealed Himself. Quietly He instructed. I waited. Silently, or so it seemed, He set the stage. Belatedly I began to catch on, or at least get an inkling, that He was moving. "Howard," He was saying to me, "I have work for you to do. Abide in me. Look for opportunities to serve. Don't be afraid. I am with you. I won't leave. I will bless you. I will give you fruit. Promise."

For three years, it seemed nothing happened. Polly and I saturated ourselves with the blessings others gave to us. We had no responsibilities. And then things began to change. Sitting, as it were, in a passenger train, we began to sense movement. Barely perceptible at first. Slowly gathering speed. Eventually reaching full speed, the Lord laid out plans for us. "Move back to Michigan. You have family there. You need them; they need you." He didn't give us any other clues. What, if anything else did He have in store for us? Dare I compare our situation to Abram's? Was God giving us a new promise? Was there a special challenge to lay aside the comforts of our Arizona home and friends, replacing them with unknown challenges and dangers? Could I physically do it?

Listen and let the record speak. Within nine months of our return, we spoke with friends about an option of starting a small group for mostly-retired people. We explored. Organized. The Lord blessed the endeavor. I cannot express the pleasure; I was back in my favorite area of ministry! And then I got the uninvited challenge of my life: become accountable with two other men in my Christian walk. I had heard of these groups. They made me nervous, at best, panicked at worst. I was definitely out of my comfort zone. God spoke. "Do it!" For over four years now we have met regularly. Like teepee poles we lean on each other. We challenge each other. Minister to each other. The Lord would have to drag me away from this experience.

I spent more time abiding in Jesus. And then I saw them. Small bunches of grapes growing on my branch. He had promised fruit; now He let me see some of it. Through a mutual friend I began an e-mail acquaintance with a fellow family physician. He has an impairment much like mine. He, too, suffers. Feels isolated. Has doubts. Makes spiritual breakthroughs. Learns to lean more on Jesus. We minister to each other.

In April, 2001, I no longer scrape any sores with the potsherd of broken dreams. I have exchanged the ash heap for a banquet table. I feast with my King. My enemies sometimes threaten the feast. Anxieties. Fears of becoming barren for Jesus. Dread of how my disease will progress. When they threaten, I look back on my past. I remember God's exhaustless grace. Then I relax in my present and confidently anticipate my future. God is not through with me; he has plans I have yet to see.

I am back. It has been a long road.

# Breakfast with Jesus
❖•❖

Sit on a large imaginary stone with me and look out over the Sea of Galilee as the sun just peeks over the horizon. Watch seven of Jesus' disciples struggle in a fishing boat (John 21). They look exhausted. Discouraged. Over and over again they had thrown the net into the sea. Over and over again they pulled it back into the boat—empty. No fish. Nothing. All night long. Their muscles screamed out from overuse. They haven't fished for years now you remember. They had given that all up to follow Jesus. Their spirits sagged below the bottom of the boat. Yesterday, they eagerly followed Peter's example. Time to go fishing! They hadn't seen Jesus in days. What else was there to do? At least they could catch fish. Or, so they thought!

Turn your gaze to the right. Peer into the distance along the edge of the lake. A solitary figure squats beside a glowing fire. It looks like he is stirring the coals. You would think he is cooking. Use the binoculars of your imagination. Focus on the fire. See fish cooking on the charcoal. See bread sitting alongside. Watch as he stands, turns toward the lake and calls out. Listen to the conversation that follows:

> *"Friends, haven't you any fish?"*
> *"No," they answered.*
> *He said, "Throw your net on the right side of the boat and you will find some." When they did, they were unable to haul the net in because of the large number of fish.*
>
> John 21:5,6

For John, it didn't take a rocket scientist to recognize this was Jesus. For Peter, it didn't require any thought to determine his action. He threw on his outer coat, jumped into the shallow water and rushed to Jesus— his Master. Following Jesus' instructions he returned to the boat, hauled in the net, and took some of the fish to Jesus. Fish that Jesus added to His. Together they produced the feast Jesus shared with these disciples.

Breakfast is over. Jesus' mission for this morning is not. Three times Jesus asked Peter if he loved Him. Three times Peter affirmed he did. Three times Jesus commissioned Peter." Feed my lambs." "Feed my sheep." "Feed my sheep." He told Peter he would die a martyr's death and then He said, "Follow me." Peter's days of fishing on the Sea of Galilee are over; his days of giving everything he has to Jesus have just begun.

Leave it to Jesus. He accepted what Peter could offer— his love and some fish. He challenged Peter. Service to others. Absolute devotion to Jesus.

. . .

Jesus calls me to my Sea of Galilee. I fish all night but cannot catch even a minnow— until He tells me where to cast my net. He asks for the fish I catch, combines them with His contribution, and provides a glorious breakfast of divine proportions. He asks for my total love for Him and repeatedly tells me to feed His sheep. He tells me to follow Him. I have not heard Him tell me where He will lead me. I have so little to offer. I am an impaired fisherman. I cannot catch a minnow without His help. My strength runs out so quickly. But, He assures me, that is adequate. He is not concerned with my limitations. My little, combined with His infinite, is more than enough!

**PART FOUR**

# The Forever Feast: Eternal Celebration and Healing of All My Disabilities

❖

*But God will redeem my life from the grave;
he will surely take me to himself.*

Ps 49:15

*... "Now God's home is with mankind!
... He will wipe away all tears from their eyes.
There will be no more death, no more grief or crying or pain.
The old things have disappeared."*

Rev 21:3-4 TEV

# Introduction: Feastmaker

❖•❖

Spin around in your chair and look back with me 2000 years.

It started out as just an ordinary wedding in an insignificant village in Galilee. Join me as we look on in our imagination. Cana was a small village. Today no one knows exactly where it was. Simple peasants lived a simple hand-to-mouth life— except for special occasions like today. Feel the excitement in the air. Today there will be a feast and much celebration. Watch the young couple, dressed in their finest, seal their vows in the wedding ceremony. Watch their neighbors escort them to their new home by the longest route possible so many can wish them well.[8]

And so the day ends. But not the celebration. Stay with me. For seven days the joyous festivity continues. But note, something is going wrong. Look at the furrows in the brow of the head waiter. Watch him study the crowd. Turn his attention to the dwindling supply of wine. The wine must last all seven days or the bride and groom will be terribly embarrassed. Supplies are getting dangerously low. Worse than that, he just now pours out the last. The final drop. There is no more. Anywhere!

The waiter is devastated. Jesus' mother, Mary, just smiles. The celebration will continue. She knows it to the depths of her soul. Her son (our Savior) will save the day, and make a feast like no one there has ever attended before. Watch her call nearby servants. Listen as she lays the problem at Jesus' feet and tells the servants to do whatever He commands. Ponder as she walks away. The problem will soon be solved.

Look at the compassion on Jesus' face. A bride and groom from a small village need rescue. Jesus gives simple directions. "Fill six jugs with water— to the very brim. Dip some out and take it to the head waiter." Just that. No fanfare.

Watch in amazement. Better yet, read for yourself what the scripture says:

> ... *The master of the banquet tasted the water that had been turned into wine. He did not realize where it had come from, though the servants who had drawn the water knew. Then he called the bridegroom aside and said, "Everyone brings out the choice wine first and then the cheaper wine after the guests have had too much to drink; but you have saved the best till now."*
> John 2:9-10.

I wonder. What do you think? Did the waiter (and the bride and groom) ever get over the astonishment of that day? How could they?

And so Jesus started His public ministry by rescuing a young couple. Think of it— His first miracle was done for the benefit of two peasants!

I believe there is more to this story. Some scholars believe the bridegroom was none other than the Apostle

John himself[9]. What a powerful boost to John's faith! Many years later, as he wrote this gospel, John must have once again thrilled at his master. Jesus, the feast maker! Jesus, provider for even the simplest people.

Whatever the history, this account boosts my faith. Jesus met the need of a young couple. Saved their day. He has met my needs over and over again. I fervently believe He will continue to do so. I will continue to feast with my Jesus—in this world and the next!

· · ·

Dejected. Dismayed. Numb. Confused. With heavy hearts Cleopas and an unnamed disciple of Jesus plod down the dusty seven miles from Jerusalem to Emmaus. Their hearts are too heavy to talk; their minds are too crammed with conflicting thoughts to keep silence. Three days ago they stared in disbelief and horror as Jesus, Master of their lives, suffered and died— victim of the Chief Priests' hatred and the Roman Government's disregard for human life. Today certain female disciples insist they have seen an angel who declares Jesus has risen from the dead. To bolster their claim, they assert the grave is empty and they have actually seen Jesus.

An uninformed stranger (Sh— we know it is Jesus) joins them. Inquires about their emotional turmoil. Calls them foolish men. Interprets to them all the scripture about the Messiah. Agrees to stay with them at their destination. Breaks bread with them. And then watch what happens. Poof; He disappears! Overwhelming! They recognize it is Jesus. Inevitable! They rush out into the night and hustle back to Jerusalem. They must find the other disciples!

Frightened beyond measure, those disciples cower in the small room. The doors are locked. Actually double bolted. What will happen to them now? Will the Jewish leaders destroy them as they did their Master? They had walked with Him for three years. Heard His teachings. Experienced changes in their very souls. But now Jesus is gone. They have lost their Master. They have also lost their way and their will. And now Cleopas and his friend have just joined them with unbelievable news. They claim they have just seen Jesus; taken bread from His hands; realized beyond all doubt it was their Master! Feel the depth of their despair, confusion, and tentative hope. Try to imagine how it would be for us if we were really in that room with them that night.

But there is more to this story! Suddenly as they heard Cleopas talk, the unbelievable happened. Don't take it from me. See it for yourself:

> *While they were still talking about this, Jesus himself stood among them and said to them, "Peace be with you." They were startled and frightened, thinking they saw a ghost. He said to them, "Why are you troubled, and why do doubts rise in your minds? Look at my hands and my feet. It is I myself! Touch me and see; a ghost does not have flesh and bones, as you see I have." When he had said this, he showed them his hands and feet. And while they still did not believe it because of joy and amazement, he asked them, "Do you have anything here to eat?" They gave him a piece of broiled fish, and he took it and ate it in their presence.*
>
> Luke 24:36-43

And then it happens! Suddenly the gloom is gone. They will never be the same again. Convinced to the center of their very souls, they will live out the rest of their lives absolutely certain of Jesus' resurrection. Totally certain that they will also live again after death and join Him forever. He offered them bread. He ate their fish. More importantly they feasted their eyes on the risen Jesus. Death lost its power! What a feast— made from two pieces of bread and one piece of fish. And Jesus.

Can two pieces of bread, one piece of fish, and Jesus make a feast? You don't need the bread or fish if Jesus is there. I know. I have feasted with him many times over many years.

...

Seventy years have passed. John has lived by faith; now Jesus is speaking to him directly. "John," Jesus is saying, "I have a new task for you. I need you to write for me." Look on with me as John contemplates the vision Jesus entrusted to him and considers the task that awaits. We look over his shoulder as he writes letters to the seven churches. Ephesus. Smyrna. Pergamum. Thyatira. Sardis. Philadelphia. Laodicea. Good news. Bad news. To every church there is a challenge. We study them all. The message to Laodicea explodes from the page. They are in big trouble. Indifferent. Satisfied. Unaware. And as we read some phrases we cringe. What hope is there for this church. Jesus said to them:

> ... *you do not realize that you are wretched, pitiful, poor, blind and naked.*
> Rev.3:17

And then to our amazement we hear Him speak in love:

> *Those whom I love I rebuke and discipline. So be earnest, and repent. Here I am! I stand at the door and knock. If anyone hears my voice and opens the door, I will come in and eat with him, and he with me.*
> Rev 3:19-20

The startling promise reverberates over the centuries: "I will come in and eat with him, and he with Me." Jesus is offering them a feast! Despite their indifference. In the face of their denial. Their blindness notwithstanding. The conditions? Repent. Accept His discipline. Open the door. The same promise, the same conditions are offered to us.

. . .

Spin your chair back around and gaze longingly into the future. There is yet another feast. This is a wedding feast like none that has ever occurred.

Forty-Seven years ago Polly and I were married and we have had three children marry; I consider myself something of an expert about preparations for the special day. Consider some of them. Who is going to do what? I mean you have to consider the officiating minister, musicians, bride's attendants, groom's attendants, flower girl, ring bearer, candle lighter, photographer. The list goes on. What happens if you forget one of the items on the list? It's enough to make a grown man cry.

Talk about preparations— the wedding I am talking about is in a league all its own. Look at what God's Word (Rev 21, 19) says about some of the preparation for the marriage of Jesus, the Lamb of God, and His bride, the church.

All of creation is changed

> *Then I saw a new heaven and a new earth, for the first heaven and the first earth had passed away, and there was no longer any sea.*
> 
> 21:1

Living conditions are totally new

> *And I heard a loud voice from the throne saying,*

> *"Now the dwelling of God is with men, and he will live with them. They will be his people, and God himself will be with them and be their God.*
>
> 21:3

Listen to this! There will be total absence of any impairment.

> *He will wipe every tear from their eyes. There will be no more death or mourning or crying or pain, for the old order of things has passed away."*
>
> 21:4

And all of this is just the preparation! The best is yet to come.

> *Then I heard what sounded like a great multitude, like the roar of rushing waters and like loud peals of thunder, shouting:*
> *"Hallelujah!*
> *For our Lord God Almighty reigns.*
> *Let us rejoice and be glad*
> *and give him glory!*
> *For the wedding of the Lamb has come,*
> *and his bride has made herself ready.*
> *Fine linen, bright and clean,*
> *was given her to wear."*
> *Then the angel said to me, "Write: 'Blessed are those who are invited to the wedding supper of the Lamb!'" And he added, "These are the true words of God."*
>
> 19: 6-9

Now, that's a wedding feast I plan to attend!

# Meditations

# The Long Hope
➤•⬅

Look back two centuries with me through the RetrospectOScope of our imagination. The aged Apostle John sits at his desk. He seems to be in deep thought. Though his face is furrowed by the passage of many years and his body scarred by torture for his faith, his eyes blaze with intensity. We listen as he muses to himself. "It has been many years," we hear him say. "It has been over sixty years since I heard my Jesus speak those words of hope:

> *In my Father's house are many rooms ... I am going there to prepare a place for you ... I will come back and take you to be with me that you also may be where I am.*
>
> John 14:1-4

He goes on in his reverie. "It has been almost that long since my brother, James, spilled his life's blood over a Roman sword. Peter, they told me, shared his Master's fate to crucifixion; Paul lost his head in a Roman dungeon. The rest of us apostles are gone. All but me. It has been a long time. A very long time."

As we continue to listen, we hear him speak of the thousands of Christians who have never seen Jesus. They will someday join Him. Enjoy His presence forever. He smiles as he remembers the ringing words that shouted out Peter's hope:

> *Praise be to the God and Father of our Lord Jesus Christ! In his great mercy he has given us new birth into a living hope through the resurrection of Jesus Christ from the dead, and into an inheritance that can never perish, spoil or fade— kept in heaven for you, who through faith are shielded by God's power until the coming of the salvation that is ready to be revealed in the last time. In this you greatly rejoice, though now for a little while you may have had to suffer grief in all kinds of trials.*
> 1 Peter 1:3-6

We look over his shoulder as he picks up his pen to write. I sense the intensity of his contemplation as he listens to hear the Master speak to him. We know without doubt he recognizes the importance of the coming words. He nods. Leans over the desk. Without hesitation inscribes each word. The message leaps from the page and into my heart.

> *... we know that when he appears, we shall be like him, for we shall see him as he is. Everyone who has this hope in him purifies himself, just as he is pure.*
> 1 John 3:2-3

I put my RetrospectOScope in its case. Sit at my desk with bowed head and heart. Begin to contemplate the meaning of those few words. My hope is real; I will be like Him.

My task is daunting; I dare not waste my time in idle waiting. Rather, I am called to holy living. Not just today, but every day. I'm in this for the long haul. As I contemplate, Jesus words leap across the centuries:

> *Be on guard! Be alert! You do not know when that time will come. It's like a man going away: He leaves his house and puts his servants in charge, each with his assigned task, and tells the one at the door to keep watch.*
> *Therefore keep watch because you do not know when the owner of the house will come back— whether in the evening, or at midnight, or when the rooster crows, or at dawn. If he comes suddenly, do not let him find you sleeping. What I say to you, I say to everyone: Watch!*
>
> Mark 13:33-37

What will be my future? What will I have to suffer? I do not know. That is not my concern. My task is to be on assignment. Today. Tomorrow. For the long hope.

# Living in Two Worlds

I live in a wonderful world. For the past few weeks the annual kaleidoscope of brilliant fall colors has smashed into my vision at every turn. Intense reds of sumac and maple. Golden yellows of oak and hickory. Persistent deep greens of hemlock— and of other leaves awaiting their turn to dress in their fall attire. Geese flying overhead honk their intention to master the airways to the south. Sandhill cranes defend their territory as they squawk in the wetlands behind our house declaring their intention to return next spring. God is preparing us for another winter. Soon we will celebrate the Christmas season with fervent devotion and festive occasions. Yes, it is a wonderful world.

I live in a terrible world. With stupefying suddenness our lives were forever changed a few weeks ago as satanic forces of hatred attacked our icons of prosperity and military power. We are learning to live in the very face of evil. Persisting smell of death at the Twin Towers in New York City. Anthrax attacks. Daily fears of other possible terrorism. Destroyed military establishments of the enemy. Unexpressible horror as we look at the faces of repressed men, women, and children every night on TV. Yes, it is a terrible world.

And both these worlds are one and the same. We are all constantly exposed to the best and the worst that coexist on planet earth. Sometimes this schizophrenic mix attacks my very core. The contrasts are too intense. My nemesis, Fatigue, strikes with fierce intensity. Mental acuity dulls. Muscular endurance dwindles. Yesterday's to-do list lies on my desk this morning mostly undone.

I lay down to rest. Fatigue begins to fade; in its place I sometimes feel an awakening longing. Someday I will not have to contend with this mixture of intense pleasure and overwhelming wretchedness. Heaven seems to beckon. Paradise reaches out to me with outstretched arms.

But wait! Not so fast! Earth is more than changes of season or travesties delivered by wicked persons. There are important people in my life— people who depend on me. There are tasks yet unfinished— tasks the Lord has challenged me with. In that moment I begin to better understand the Apostle Paul:

> *For to me, to live is Christ and to die is gain. If I am to go on living in the body, this will mean fruitful labor for me. Yet what shall I choose? I do not know! I am torn between the two ...*
> Phil 1:20-23

There is yet more. I find I am seeking heaven to lose suffering. Gain rest. The motives somehow seem inferior. But, as I struggle the Lord speaks:

> *Then I heard a voice from heaven say, "Write: Blessed are the dead who die in the Lord from now on." "Yes," says the Spirit, "they will rest from*

*their labor, for their deeds will follow them."*
                                    Rev 14:13

   Fatigue fades. Uncertainty vanishes. I am not made for earth alone. God did not create me only for heaven. I am a citizen of both. I reach out my arms to grasp the whole.

# Expectation

The title jumps off the page of my memory just as it jumped off the page of the program from a missions seminar many years ago: "Preparation for the 'Unpreparable.'" We eagerly sought to know what to expect as new missionaries. We listened. We discussed. In the end we discovered we could never really know until we actually experienced missionary life. Expectation is just a shadow of realization.

For many weeks I have tried to wrap my mind around my current assignment. Studied. Prayed. Thought. What is heaven going to be like? What am I going to be like in heaven? Even scripture is largely quiet. It tantalizes me. Whets my interest. Leaves me with unanswered questions. Join me as we review some of those snippets of divine truth:

> *However, as the scripture says,*
> *"What no one ever saw or heard,*
> *what no one ever thought could happen,*
> *is the very thing God prepared for those who love him."*
>
> 1 Cor 2:9 TEV

Paul teases us as he reviews his experience.

*I know a man in Christ who fourteen years ago was caught up to the third heaven. Whether it was in the body or out of the body I do not know-God knows. And I know that this man- whether in the body or apart from the body I do not know, but God knows- was caught up to paradise. He heard inexpressible things, things that man is not permitted to tell.*

2 Cor 12:2-4

And he summarizes the whole.

*Now we see but a poor reflection as in a mirror; then we shall see face to face. Now I know in part; then I shall know fully, even as I am fully known.*

1 Cor 13:12

What, I prayed, can I write that will bring hope to those who suffer and long for relief? What, Lord, do You say to me as I suffer? Then that message from long ago crashed into my current reality. My brain shouted, "Remember, expectation is but a shadow of realization." No matter how I perceive heaven I will come up short. My thoughts will be far too small.

Pain will be gone. But that is too small an expectation. Somehow God will do more than just erase past anguish. Inexpressible fatigue. Terrible torment. Dare I guess what that "more that just" will be? I have tried. Recalled the best health I have ever experienced. Relived the fastest race I ever ran. Remembered the greatest ecstacy I ever knew. All of that disappears in the reality of the new me that God will create.

CNS  JD5Q1A

# BUSINESS REPLY MAIL
FIRST-CLASS MAIL     PERMIT NO 304     HARLAN IA

POSTAGE WILL BE PAID BY ADDRESSEE

**ConsumerReports**®

SUBSCRIPTION DEPARTMENT
PO BOX 2100
HARLAN IA 51593-2289

NO POSTAGE
NECESSARY
IF MAILED
IN THE
UNITED STATES

# ConsumerReports®

## 1 YEAR FOR $94.66

**YOUR PRICE $29**

Subscribe to *Consumer Reports* for 1 year (12 issues) and save 69% off the cover price. PLUS receive the *Buying Guide 2015* FREE.

Name _____ (please print)

Address _____ Apt. _____

City _____ State _____ Zip _____

☐ Payment enclosed (use an envelope)
(Please make check payable to: Consumer Reports)

☐ Bill me

**ORDER ONLINE:** www.ConsumerReports.org/cr/sub

JD5Q1A

PRINT + iPAD ACCESS

**Subscribers:** Please allow 4 to 8 weeks for delivery. Rate is for the U.S. only. Savings off newsstand price. If the Post Office alerts us that your magazine is undeliverable, we have no further obligation unless we receive a corrected address within two years.

To access our Privacy Policy and learn more about your privacy rights, go to ConsumerReports.org/privacy

*Dear friends, now we are children of God, and what we will be has not yet been made known. But we know that when he appears, we shall be like him, for we shall see him as he is.*
1 John 3:2

In the presence of this great declaration all I can say is, "Wow." All I can do is fall on my face before the Lamb of God who said:

*... "I am making everything new!" ... "It is done. I am the Alpha and the Omega, the Beginning and the End. To him who is thirsty I will give to drink without cost from the spring of the water of life. He who overcomes will inherit all this, and I will be his God and he will be my son."*
Rev 21:5-7

# The Forever Feast

For weeks I have had a recurring dream that I had arrived in heaven. Over time the dream has enlarged. Expanded. Come to possess much of my waking thoughts. Sleeping dreams blend with waking contemplation.

Heaven! The ultimate goal. My final destination. Culmination of much of my adult life's desire. My experiences overwhelm my ability to contain them. Allow me to share with you.

I swung around to take my first look of the celestial landscape. Awesome! Indescribable. Think back to the promise He made in His Holy Word:

> *However, as it is written: "No eye has seen, no ear has heard, no mind has conceived what God has prepared for those who love him."*
> 1Cor 2:9

Allow me to exercise my imagination. Expand my dream. As I gazed dumbfounded, I saw a mighty stream of Living Water cascading down to me. The water is clearer, purer, more mighty than the magnificent mountain streams high in the Colorado Rockies I knew as a child. Something inside compelled me to stoop, fill my hands, drink deeply. I cannot describe this water. I cannot relate what I experienced. And then it happened. Suddenly I realized I was stooping without any assistance. I have not been able to do that for years!

In my dream, I stood. I was captivated by magnificent trees standing stately and tall on either side of the river. Each tree was filled to its very top with thousands of fruit. I heard the Lord's voice. "This, My son, is the Tree of Life. Pick. Eat. Live forever. With Me." I gazed upward standing on very tiptoe. Danced around the tree as gracefully as the greatest of ballet dancers. Stretched for the highest fruit. Reached out and clutched it to my breast. Sank my teeth into the very essence of eternal life. Once again I was awestruck. I stood on tiptoe unaided. Gazed upward. Without losing my balance. Reality breaks into my reverie. How long has it been since I performed that feat?

Glancing sideways without double vision (not experienced for ever-so-long on earth) my attention fell on a booth of the Celestial Wireless Communication System. There is someone I must find. For years I had thought about him. Contemplated meeting him. Yearned to run down heaven's streets with him. Longed to share Heaven's cuisine with him. I ran to the booth. "Mephibosheth," I called, "Join me at Heaven's gate. I have just arrived. I need to see Jesus. Fall at His feet. Bathe His hands and feet with my tears of joy and gratitude. I want to race with you to the Wedding Supper of the Lamb and sit with you at His table. We can feast forever!"

# Notes

1. The Electromyogram (EMG) measures the electrical activity of a muscle using a fine needle inserted in the muscle.
2. Magnetic resonance imaging (MRI) produces an electronic image of the tested area. The patient lies in a long narrow instrument often called "The Tunnel."
3. American Heritage Dictionary of the English Language, Third Edition (Electronic Version), Boston: Houghton Mifflin Company (1996).
4. Lehman, H.S., Nothing But Leaves (copyright Lehman Gottschling, renewed 1952, Assigned to Singspiration, Inc.).
5. "Message in a Bottle," (Burbank California: Warner Bros., 1999).
6. Dr. Darold L. Hill, Senior Pastor, Spring Arbor Free Methodist Church, Spring Arbor Michigan.
7. Starring Robert Redford and adapted from the novel of the same name by Nicholis Evans.
8. An excellent description of Jewish marriage customs is given in William Barclay's Daily Study Bible

Series, (Philadelphia: Westminster Press, 1975) in the commentary on John 2:1-11.
9. Adam Clarke's Commentary, Electronic Database (Seattle: Biblesoft, 1996) commentary on John 2:1.